"It's about his needs. His addiction. He has to keep killing to feel any satisfaction. Or maybe he's being told what to do," Tally answered firmly, glaring into Cid's blue eyes, eyes that had seen too much.

"His mother?"

With a sudden new clarity Tally shook her head. "Yes. She could be just as ruthless, just as addicted," she said, finally giving verbal credence to the thought. It sounded weak to her, yet it had a certain plausibility.

"You know, all the years I worked homicide I've seen husbands kill their wives, children kill their parents, wives stab their husbands, but I never understood what kind of mother kills." Cid's voice was soft, yet it suggested a deeper tension.

Tally apprised her, "Given the right circumstances, anyone is capable of anything."

A simple phrase, Cid thought, that held a deeper meaning. In a world gone nuts with violence, no one could be trusted.

Visit

Bella Books

at

BellaBooks.com

or call our toll-free number

1-800-729-4992

A Tally McGinnis Mystery

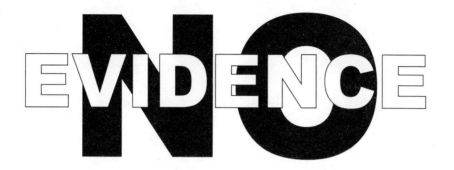

NANCY SANRA

Bella
BOOKS
2005

Bella Books, Inc.
P.O. Box 10543
Tallahassee, FL 32302

Printed in the United States of America on acid-free paper
First Edition

Editor: Anna Chinappi
Cover designer: Sandy Knowles

ISBN 1-59493-043-0

For Sherry
I looked at my heart and you were written there forever.

And for Janet, my very special sister

About the Author

Nancy Sanra and her partner, Sherry, live in the beautiful Pioneer Valley at the foot of the Berkshire Mountains in Western Massachusetts. Besides writing four Tally McGinnis mysteries, Nancy also writes children's books for kids with special needs and is in the process of completing a mystery series for young adults. A graduate of the University of California, Nancy is a retired regional sales director and now writes full-time. Both Nancy and Sherry enjoy hiking with their wonderful dog Snickers and quiet evenings shared with good friends.

Nancy welcomes e-mail at NSanra@aol.com and reminds you to always follow your dream.

Prologue
Thursday, July 4
8:21 p.m.

As red and blue rockets burst in the night sky, Gertrude Rogers stood by a closed doorway that led into a corridor running the length of her home. A still-handsome woman of eighty-three, she had once been an energetic figure. Now her brown eyes were fixed gloomily on the door, her thin and frail hands cupped over her nose.

Somebody loves me, I wonder who, I wonder who.

Like the sick, putrid smell that enveloped her house, she could not escape the song. She heard the tune in her sleep. Over the din of her television. When she ate or prayed. Shivering from a fear that never left her, the old woman stood silent, her weight shifting from one foot to the other. She knew better than to enter the long hallway. She knew better than to complain. In the past her fingers were broken when she disobeyed the rules. But tonight, despite her fear, she would have her moment.

Gertrude folded her arms. Her voice rose, quivering. "The smell is bad again."

Her lips pulled back as if her skin were shrinking and aging as she spoke. In an effort to steady herself, she reached for a white wicker chair next to the door, taking time to feel the exhalation of her defiance. "Fix the stench."

Down the corridor, an open doorway to the right led to a small cell-like cavity. The odor that seeped from inside was distinctive. The rancid smell of death and decay. It hung in the air and crawled into the dark crevices like the fog outside.

Startled by Gertrude's rigid voice, his eyes darted toward the hall. He frowned, his serried eyebrows becoming one solid line. The expression suggested a slow-burning rage. He disdained insubordination.

Cautiously he listened, glanced back at the door, adrenaline burning. "She'll deal with you later," he whispered flatly. The words, his morbid thoughts, seemed to energize him.

With a faint smile his lower lip twitched and his rich baritone voice gathered intensity. *Somebody loves me, I wonder who; I wonder who.*

Carefully he adjusts an intense concentrated beam from an ancient overhead surgical light. The illumination revealed a cold space with unpainted stucco walls, rough and dotted with dark splotches that appeared to be old, dry blood. There is evidence of scraping and sanding as if an intense effort had been made to remove the stains. He likes things clean and organized.

Beneath a curtained window that overlooks tall grass is a carefully crafted wooden platform with the nude body of a young woman on top. To the right, draped across an old gray office chair, is a pink blouse. It is slit from hem to collar.

A simple pride seems to register on his face as he bends over the hapless body. Rigor mortis has long gone. He has kept his trophy for weeks, sometimes in an old refrigerator that sits in the corner, sometimes in the cold room.

Masterfully he maneuvers an arm and carefully sets a surgical towel in place. Each movement is specific. A well-choreographed ritual. Proudly he closes his steel gray eyes and allows himself to recall her voice, her pleas, her cries. Aroused and elated, he again smiles.

Somebody loves me, I wonder who, I wonder who.

He is breathing hard now. "This is the night," he says triumphantly, putting everything else out of his mind except for the task that lies before him. His gloved fingers reach for a new disposable scalpel as he begins the first of many neat incisions.

Chapter One
Wednesday, September 16
9:06 a.m.

"He kidnapped, raped, and killed her," Dana Haskall began in nervous shaky sentences. Oblivious to the onlookers waiting for the elevator, she gazed at her hands. Her face was deeply lined, her somber brown eyes filled with grief. "And then he left her in a field all alone. My baby daughter. My best friend."

Pressed forward by the crowd, they entered the elevator. Dana folded her arms, her eyes pleading for support. She was tall and well dressed and carried an expensive leather purse. She also wore a Rolex that cost more than Tally made on most cases.

A FedEx delivery man, arms filled with two large boxes and a clipboard, leaned forward trying to hear more details.

"I saw your picture in the paper. I could tell you were warm and understanding. I need your help."

Filled with unease, Tally felt at once the weight of this stranger's pain. Then she asked, "Who killed your daughter?"

Dana bit her lip. "I don't know. That's why I'm here."

The elevator stopped on the tenth floor of the office complex that served as the home of the Phoenix Detective Agency. Silently, Tally led the tormented woman into a spacious and tastefully furnished suite with floor-to-ceiling windows, which provided a panoramic view of San Francisco.

Wearing her authority naturally, Tally ran the detective agency with skill and wit. She was a strong woman, opinionated and at times bossy, yet an inherent kindness kept her from being overbearing.

Guiding Dana Haskall to her private office, Tally sat beside her on a soft black leather couch. The distraught mother shifted her weight back and snuggled tightly in the corner, rocking back and forth, despairingly searching for consolation. Slowly she explained that her only child was found dead two months earlier.

"I'm a single mother." Eyes averted, Dana pushed her fingers through her jet-black hair, which was shoulder length and graying at the temples. "I *was* a single mother," she corrected. "I'm on a leave of absence from my clothing business until this matter . . . until my daughter's murder is avenged."

Briefly, Tally touched Dana's hand. She knew the only kindness at this moment was silence.

Once more, Dana turned her head, as if the human touch was more than she could bear. "Johanna was her name. She was just twenty. A brilliant music major at San Jose State. She was a child prodigy. Piano was her genius, as was composition. She was so refined and so beautiful. Her first major concert was scheduled for December with the New York Philharmonic. Carnegie Hall."

Abruptly, Dana stood, pushed by sorrow. "They found her up north about eighty miles from here. A small beach community. I've never seen her. Both my attorney and the medical examiner advised against it." She spoke matter-of-factly. "They said she had been dead quite some time when she was found. I'm told decomposition can be ugly." Her voice trailed off.

"Johanna had been missing for weeks. I knew she was dead long before they found her. She was too responsible not to have called me, and she never would have missed her classes. My fervent prayer is that she wasn't tortured and didn't suffer." Her hands were shaking now.

Filled with empathy as well as curiosity, Tally stood and crossed the room. She poured a glass of water from a Waterford pitcher and offered it to Dana Haskall. "How can I help you?"

Running her index finger around the edge of her glass, Dana hesitated, her expression composed and her voice mild. "The article about you in the *Chronicle* stated that your mother had been in a semi-coma for the past several months. The results of a violent act by an unknown malefactor. I sympathize with you and offer hope for her recovery," she responded in an even softer voice.

Facing Tally, her gaze was one of total compassion. "Because of your mother's condition I knew you more than anyone else would understand what I am going through. The sheriff's office in Coast County seems almost indifferent to Johanna's death. The only suspect I'm aware of cried harassment and was released immediately by the chief at the local police department in Goldenrod. Now they all seem less than eager to pursue whatever clues they might have. And poor Johanna still hasn't had a proper burial. I want to hire your firm to hunt down this rapist, this wretched individual, and to give me back my daughter so I may put her to rest." She rubbed her stomach, the antacid she had taken earlier in the morning no longer working.

The light from the window played shadowy tricks on the wall. Dana touched the corner of Tally's large oak desk. Normally she wasn't a woman to make demands on someone's working style. "And you must promise me, regardless of how painful your investigation may be, you will hold nothing back and keep me informed at all times."

Dana sipped her glass of water, studying Tally over the rim.

Tally nodded, noticing Dana did not wear a wedding ring. "And Johanna's father?"

A sharp look was quickly checked by a deeper emotion. "*I* am contracting the Phoenix Detective Agency. Her father is not involved, and I do not wish him contacted."

Tally kneaded her temples and patiently explained, "Most homicides are committed by friends or family. Talking to all relatives is well-advised in a case of this nature."

There was something nasty in Dana Haskall's eyes, a darker quality. She straightened her back. "Johanna's father is *not* to be contacted."

Chapter Two
Wednesday, September 16
10:15 a.m.

Midmorning sunlight floated through the expansive windows, touched the loose brown ringlets of Katie O'Neil's shoulder-length hair, and came to rest on the corner of her highly polished mahogany desk.

When Tally first met her she had thought Katie was a perfect office manager. She kept to herself and took care of business. Tally also found her to be a lovely, trim, blue-eyed woman, with delicate features bathed in good humor. Now, seven years later, she was the beautiful center of Tally's life who viewed love as a gift and passion as a tender reward. She brought understanding and insight to their relationship, nurtured a love of beauty, and laughed with an intimacy that put everyone at ease.

Moving closer, Tally kissed her on the nape of her neck. "I'll be back later," she whispered.

Tucking the receiver under her chin, Katie held up a finger as she spoke into the phone, her Irish lilt harboring a bit of mischief.

"Aye, tis very important the table be next to the window overlooking the bay. And be sure the wine steward has a bottle of Grand Annee champagne chilled, as we'll be wanting that as soon as we arrive."

Long on charm and with a lively mind, Katie was as strong as she was lovely, and she took her partnership in the Phoenix Detective Agency seriously. Managing the office filled her life with interest and challenge, and, if not a hundred percent enthused with Tally's long hours and obsession with her work, Katie was at least tolerant. She understood homicide was Tally's talent. Vindicator versus victimizer.

For Tally, although her heart was filled with the love of Katie, her head wasn't always as wise. She allowed herself to be consumed by cases and to push relentlessly for resolution. She wanted cons nailed and killers locked up. And there was the recent frustration and guilt surrounding her mother. A deep fear within her that dated back two months, a feeling she was responsible for the beating her mother had gotten at the hands of a serial killer she should have taken off the streets. When she closed her eyes she still saw her mother's frightened features, and when she awoke in the night her skin was damp with fear. Now, even more obsessed, she sought out the solution of other cases in an attempt to keep the guilt from swallowing her whole.

As Katie saw Tally watching her, a faint smile appeared and she gently winked. Her face was an infinite resource of expressions: smiles, frowns, smirks, tiny pouts.

So strange, Katie thought, to want someone so deeply for so long that sometimes you cannot believe you actually have them to love. If Tally found satisfaction for her life in her job, Katie O'Neil found it in her love for Tally.

Putting down the telephone, she leaned over and brushed her lips against Tally's. "Our dinner reservations are for seven this evening at Angels by the Sea. Please be on time."

As if some private thought amused her, Tally smiled. Her eyes warmed as she thought seriously about grabbing Katie and taking her back to the conference room where there was a nine-foot couch, but instead she brought her mouth to Katie's and allowed it to linger. "New case," she said at length, "got to run."

Katie briefly smiled at her. "You had carnal mischief on your mind." She raised her eyebrows, flirting.

Letting the temptation wash over her again, Tally fondly glanced at Katie. "Like they say, a good lay is a great way to start the day."

"You're full of pure blather, Tally McGinnis. Now off with you and don't you be forgetting, seven o'clock." Katie seemed to gauge Tally's strength of will.

Cupping her face in her hands, Tally lightly touched her lips to Katie's forehead. For a moment, Tally's green eyes held the warmth of love. Then she thought of Dana Haskall and felt herself stiffen. Adrenaline hit her bloodstream. "I have to go. See you at seven."

Chapter Three
Wednesday, September 16
12:42 p.m.

It was raining in Goldenrod, not a downpour, just intermittent showers with patches of blue sky and sun hanging low on the horizon. Labor Day weekend had come and gone, and in its wake Indian summer arrived, leaving a blanket of unusually sticky, hot weather that clung along the West Coast from Fort Bragg to Coos Bay.

Four miles away in town, most of the summer businesses were shut down for the season, and the locals were busy storing beach paraphernalia and painting and repairing for the next tourist onslaught.

Had the task at hand not been ringed with prevailing evil, Tally would have found the solitude of the Pacific Ocean refreshing and the floral array of Goldenrod both captivating and beautiful.

Just off Highway 1, the kidney-shaped piece of land known as Hughes Cove was hidden from view by dozens of thick, looming fir and pine trees. The dirt path that led to the bluff was narrow and deeply shadowed and in places overgrown with underbrush. The coastline was a quiet stretch of sand and rock. Because there was no beach access, the land was nearly always deserted. Hughes Cove's only claim to fame was a decent view of the lighthouse a half a mile offshore.

Tall and rangy, Tally stood on the edge of the steep precipice overlooking the breaking waves. She projected a silent strength—lean, fit, feminine but unmistakably able-bodied. Swirling wind tossed her short coppery bob as she lifted her binoculars and surveyed the wooded roadside, undulant sandy turf, and long tentacles of slimy seaweed that clung to the jagged rocks below. Each detail about her, from her clear complexion and blithe smile to the hint of pale shadow on her eyes, reflected Tally's style.

"A lot of people escape the Bay Area and come up here on weekends." Tally paused, breathed deeply, and glanced at Dana Haskall. "Salt air, sea breezes, and beach strolling for the overworked and stressed. When I was little my mother and father brought me to the cliffs to fly kites. The ocean was magic."

She could remember every detail, the wind, the sky, the way her father had once grinned with her delight. And her mother, her dear mother. The two beloved people that had helped make her who she was. Both had been victims of violence, her father murdered, her mother savagely beaten, and now Tally's smile that had once come so easily was seldom seen. Tally looked away, mentally centered herself, then silently turned back.

As she tilted her head slightly, Dana Haskall's face seemed to reflect some distant, pleasant memory of her own, and then the sadness returned. When Dana spoke a hardness crept into her voice. "The medical examiner told me Johanna's arms were oddly positioned, and strangely, the two opal rings her grandmother had given her were still on her fingers."

"With sex slayings I could see one of the rings being taken as a souvenir, but robbery would be uncommon. The motive is usually something more insidious. And if the killer does take something, it's usually a trophy, like underwear, a lock of hair, an ear or finger."

Conflicted, Tally exhaled deeply. She saw the tight look in Dana's full face, saw her slump a little and for a moment considered ending the conversation, but she could also sense Dana's need for honesty, and she had promised when she took the case to be straightforward. Tentatively she continued. "The perp probably killed Johanna either for enjoyment or because he was trying to hide something."

As she was stung by the gravity of Tally's words, Dana's head dropped. Her body seemed to slump a little more. She said, "Please go on."

Opening her black pocket notebook, like so many times before, Tally took notes of every detail and sketched anything of significance. Inevitably, each image was locked into her memory. By the time they left the scene, Dana's initial contact to the position of the body would be recorded. There would be no mistakes, no missing evidence. Measurements would be taken, cause of death described in detail.

"Did Johanna live on campus in a dorm?"

"No. She rented a little house. She needed room for her baby grand and the freedom to practice whenever she liked. Last fall a friend of hers was going to England on scholarship, Oxford, and wanted to sublet. We snatched it up immediately. The house is only about a mile from the music department. Johanna used to ride her bike back and forth."

A wave broke loudly on the shore a hundred feet below. The tide was slowly coming in and the rain had stopped. The view was spectacular, but there was an eerie loneliness about the area.

"She didn't have a car?" Tally asked.

"Oh, yes, a blue Volvo, but she seldom used it on campus. Usually just to come home to San Francisco on an occasional weekend. Even then she fussed about driving. That's why I thought it particularly strange that her car was found here parked along the road. I can't imagine her driving from San Jose."

As she scrutinized the path that rose gently up the hill, Tally felt the familiar challenge, the anger crawling under her skin, the hatred for whatever monster had killed Johanna Haskall.

She appeared calm yet determined. Questions shot through her mind. *How had Johanna's body gotten here? Did she know her killer? How had she died? And why had the killer brought her to the lonely plateau just outside of a chic tourist village?*

"Did Johanna have a boyfriend or girlfriend? Or did she mention someone who may have been obsessed with her, may have been stalking her?"

Ignoring the dampness of her trench coat and dark hair, Dana spoke in a combination of impatience and sorrow. "The sheriff told me there was no indication her death was linked to her personal life. Johanna was a musician and most of her free time was spent practicing or composing. Certainly she dated men, but there was no one person in her life and absolutely no time to be spent prattling around the beach."

She gave a stabbing glance. "And for the record, her friends were sophisticates, not murderers."

"Killers are killers. Undereducated or PhDs. Rich or poor."

Turning, Dana eyed Tally critically, further signaling her annoyance. "The sheriff also said there were no clues out here.

14

Apparently the local police chief moved the body before the medical examiner arrived. All evidence may have been lost."

Sudden images of the poster boy smooth-faced sheriff flickered in Dana's mind. This time when she spoke she seemed less tense. "The sheriff said this was the cleanest crime scene he had ever seen. Aren't you wasting your time, our time, with this redundancy?"

Tally did not answer and did not need to. Having once been a crack inspector for the San Francisco Police Department, she only partially accepted the fact that no evidence was likely to be found on a cold crime scene. Long ago she had learned to trust her unflagging grasp of detail and shrewd attention to nuance. She wasn't about to be scared off by the passage of time or the workings of a sick, clever killer.

Grim and suddenly restless, she turned abruptly, nearly knocking Dana Haskall to the ground.

A faint flush appeared on Tally's cheeks. "I'm so sorry. You're not hurt?"

A small shrug from Dana dismissed the question as unimportant. "Are you finding anything? Do you have any hunches or theories? Do you even care that my daughter has been raped and murdered?" Her pleas were accompanied by glances through pathetic bloodshot eyes.

Silent, Tally winced. The burden of Dana's despair darkened her thoughts. She hated murder, and its purposeless presence was constantly in her mind. It was also a frustrating aspect of her profession that grieving parents or lovers often struck out at her because she could not instantly provide answers for the unanswerable. In their moments of grief, the other victims didn't understand that Tally, that no one, was capable of erasing the nightmare of murder.

She brushed back the fine ends of her coppery hair. Despite her discomfort at having Johanna's mother at the crime scene,

Tally knew Dana not only had a right to be there, but for her peace of mind needed to know someone was doing something to solve the cruel death of her only child.

Respecting that Dana was both grieving and stressed, Tally spoke in a familiar combination of logic and caring. "This is not an open-and-shut case, and I'm not about to rely on someone else's investigation to try to find answers. You deserve better."

Taking in the death scene with a glance, Tally explained with simple kindness, "We just started. Contrary to what you may have seen on television, murder investigation is a step-by-step process. If we're lucky the perp makes an obvious mistake at the time the crime is committed and resolution is quick." She waved her hand. Her yellow rain slicker flapped in the wind. "This is an old crime scene. It's going to take time."

Tally chose not to mention that the likelihood of solving the case decreases with each passing day.

Studying Dana, Tally saw both her anger and pain. Lightly, she squeezed her arm. "I do care about your daughter, and I will do everything I can to find her killer."

She waited in silence for a moment, touching the loop of her gold earring. "Did Johanna live alone?"

"No. Her roommate, Sissy . . ." Dana looked up and for the first time a simple smile crossed her face. "Carolina Childs is a sophomore studying violin. She grew up on a watermelon farm in Dothan, Alabama, and her family has called her Sissy since she was born. A million freckles, fiery red hair and a personality to match, but my goodness, what a talent. She'll end up at Juilliard soon. She and Johanna were close friends. I'm sure Sissy will speak to you if you desire. She's still living at the house in San Jose."

Tally's brow furrowed. "I'll need the address." A glint of sunlight caused Tally to raise her hand and shield her eyes. She pulled her sunglasses off the top of her head and slid them on. "How was Johanna killed?"

Unwittingly, Dana reached for her neck, straining to comprehend. "Strangulation by ligature, the sheriff said."

"Body was up here. What the hell you lookin' at down there?" Pointing impatiently, Cid Cameron stepped forward, her rumpled navy Dockers gathering spatters of sand on the back of her legs as she walked toward an area still cordoned off by bright yellow crime scene tape.

An opinionated woman of fifty-five, she was the exact opposite of Tally's image, pulpy and rumpled with a thatch of unruly gray hair. By reputation, Cid had been a formidable homicide lieutenant in San Francisco before hitting the thirty-year mark and opting for a pension and a little less stress by joining Tally as one-third owner of the Phoenix Detective Agency. Her years of dealing with sleazebags and cold-blooded killers had brought wisdom to her pudgy face, but also an undeniable sadness to her pale blue eyes. She had been lead investigator in thirty-nine homicides. The smell of violent death clung to her nostrils as if she were born with it, and the portraits of mutilated bodies marched across her dreams nightly. She was an old-school detective, Humphrey Bogart with tits.

Normally the title of homicide lieutenant was just a career hesitation, a step on the way to upper management or even chief. But Cid came from an era when a woman cop had to be crude, crass, and fast on her feet in order to be accepted by the rank and file. Polishing her public persona was the least of her worries, and in the end it cost her any advancement.

Still, she missed her tough, old cop surroundings. The days and nights of gray nicotine-stained cubicles where sleep deprivation was a way of life, and solving murders was the only recreation any good career cop understood. Yet she loved working with Tally, and despite their differences in appearance and social outlook, they had a bond, a mutual respect for each other and a friendship that was familiar and trusting.

Tally took long purposeful strides around a large boulder

and up a slight incline. The orange and red autumn goldenrod bent slightly in the wind and brushed against her neatly pressed khakis as she carefully watched where she walked. Her green eyes were calm yet preoccupied, devouring every inch of ground looking for any evidence that might have survived the wind and rain, the curious, even the police and forensic unit.

"There's no tire tracks." Tally hesitated, shaking her head. "You would think if Johanna was murdered here there would be some sign. Broken flowers. Maybe some crushed weeds and sand kicked around. Other than a little matted grass, there's nothing. No hint of frenzy." She paused for emphasis. "And definitely no sign Johanna put up a struggle. And the road is what, half a mile away. That's a long way to tote a body if she was killed someplace else and dumped here."

Tally spun in the sand, facing Dana. "How tall was Johanna, and how much did she weigh?"

"A little over five feet and about a hundred, at most a hundred and three pounds."

Tally heaved a sigh, straightened, and took a sideways glance toward the road. "If our killer was strong, he could have carried her here."

"At this point, the condition of the ground or the vegetation doesn't mean jack shit," Cid shot back, patting herself down for cigarettes. "Hell, for all we know every beachcomber in California has trampled here since the victim was found."

She pointed with an unlit Virginia Slim at the ground. "I agree if this is the primary crime scene we should see some damage. Dead grass. Dead flowers. Tire tracks from the M.E.'s van. But look at the amount of time that has passed, Tal. Who the hell knows what the wind has blown away or for that matter, what some sicko tourist has picked up and taken home for a souvenir."

Pondering for a moment, Cid fixed her eyes on Tally. "As far as the body being dumped . . ." She shrugged, played with the idea. "You could be on to something."

Respectfully, Cid turned to Dana Haskall, her eyes flat yet friendly. "This is gonna get a little rough. You sure you want to hear it all?"

Feeling frightened and alone, Dana swallowed, her eyes filling with determination. Head bowed, she silently nodded.

Sorting through her thoughts, Cid got down on all fours to examine the small cordoned-off area more closely. She jammed her cigarette in her mouth and lit it.

"Sickos that rape and murder like to take their time. It's part of their ritual to play with their victims. This is how they get their gratification, their feeling of power. And as much as they don't want to be caught, they don't want to be interrupted in the middle of their little dance either. They are shrewd and intelligent and good talkers. They know how to manipulate the cautious, gain trust, and snatch most anyone they want. I'd bet this killer kept Johanna alive for days or weeks and then dumped her out here when she no longer could or would comply with his wishes."

Turning away, Dana Haskall shuddered; her eyes misted. "Will we ever know what really happened to Johanna?"

Tally absorbed Dana's anguish, knowing how desperately she needed assurance. But she also knew the brutal truth— there was no certainty, no promise of resolution when it came to murder. From the notorious, like Ted Bundy, to the relatively unknown slayer on death row, most took their ghoulish secrets to the grave.

Awkwardly pushing her bulk to a standing position, Cid probed the grass with her foot, then looked Dana squarely in the eye. "Some things are best left unknown."

Tally drew in a deep breath and looked again at the small bushes and plants. Her mood seemed to lighten. She removed her rain slicker, exposing a gold and red Forty-niner sweatshirt. "According to lore, Scottish houses and fields are surrounded with goldenrod to protect against evil curses. Did you know that?"

In the sun's glare Cid's face looked tight, her jaw muscles flexing. With a faint smile, she gave Tally an ironic glance and wiped her face on her wrinkled white shirtsleeve. Along with a gush of smoke, an amused chuckle seeped from the corner of her mouth, the cynical snicker that comes from having seen too much unpleasantness.

"Only thing the Scots ever got right was the recipe for good booze. No frilly flowers ever kept evil away." Her blue eyes paled under her bushy gray eyebrows as she pointed at the yellow crime scene tape and the white spray painted outline of Johanna Haskall's body.

Somebody loves me, I wonder who, I wonder who.

He let his eyes close as he slowly traced an *S* over her left breast and across the nipple. "You're trembling," he whispered.

He pushed his finger into her deep, soft flesh until she cried out.

"Shut up, bitch."

With a sense of ritualistic glee he walked around her, tightened the shackles. "I like your size and shape. And your eyes," he said, touching her porcelain white cheek, "are beautiful. I love blue."

"Please, let me go," she begged. Tears rolled down her smudged cheeks and dripped from her chin.

He grabbed her breast and squeezed hard, his mouth a cynical sneer. "I told you to shut up. You have to follow the rules, otherwise it will upset her. You only speak when I tell you or you will pay."

He reached for a new scalpel and traced two intersecting

lines across her breasts. Blood ran freely down her stomach and into her pubic hair.

Her tears flowed faster. She sucked in her breath but did not scream.

"Good." He smiled. "A little late, but you are learning."

Somebody loves me, I wonder who, I wonder who.

Chapter Four
Wednesday, September 16
2:35 p.m.

Turning east off the highway Tally drove toward central Goldenrod, the hills rising sharply against the blue-gray sky. A mile later she nosed her red BMW into a metered parking spot. Dana Haskall pulled in beside her.

The day had brought a gauntness to Dana's face, and the lines along her forehead were deeper and her eyes darker. Flatly, she got out of her blue Jaguar and handed Tally Carolina Childs's San Jose address and a picture of the victim.

Tally breathed loudly. The young woman in the picture was as lovely as her mother had described. Her face had a simple prettiness: sculpted cheekbones, wide-set brown eyes that glinted with determination. She had long, glossy black hair.

"I'm heading back to San Francisco now. I'll wait to hear from you." Dana's voice sounded tight and tired as she turned away. Once more, Tally was struck by the depth of her despair.

She felt the tension leave her body as she watched the grieving woman's car slowly drive away. For a quiet moment Tally gazed out the window, the ocean in the distance a midnight blue, the autumn sun low in the cloudy sky. A fishing boat silently drifted by.

Stiff from sitting, Cid thrust the door open and pushed out of the BMW. To her east, old-growth woods climbed the hills, reminding her that at one time this area had been a thriving monument to the timber industry. To the west, between the highway and the ocean, a pumpkin patch gave birth to little dots of orange. The air was filled with the scent of daisies, and California poppies sprang from the cracks in the sidewalk.

She jammed her hands in her pants pockets and turned to Tally. "Nice little town. I could live here."

"You and a couple of million for a house," Tally said, as she joined Cid on the sidewalk. She spread her arms, trying to absorb some ultraviolet rays. Two kids on bicycles rushed by and waved.

The little town of Goldenrod was two blocks long. A safe, family-oriented community free of litter and smog. The commercial buildings were mostly old brick, the businesses new and trendy. On one side of the street, a coffeehouse, a half a dozen cozy restaurants, some with chairs and colorful umbrella-covered tables, and three chic clothing stores. On the other side, an artsy movie theater, an ice cream stand called the Pink Pelican, and a couple of antique stores. The Cork and Bottle, a wine shop and yuppie favorite, sat at the crossroads next to a dingy white building that had once been the office for the old sawmill. Now, the wooden sign out front simply read Police Department. There were several large warehouses behind the police station and a one-story brick building surrounded by red geraniums that housed the town offices. The whole village could be seen in about an hour.

Homes near the water tended to be newer and sold for millions. Blue-collar houses inland were older, somewhat run-down, and affordable.

Once Labor Day weekend passed, the streets of Goldenrod were usually empty. The fisherman, lumberjacks, and other locals hung out in a few dimly lit bars that were off the beaten path and definitely out of sight. Most of the twelve hundred residents were of the working class who stuck to themselves and rarely raised hell. There were no schools, so children were bused fifteen miles, and the tiny police department was home to one appointed official named Fred Peterson, who had been the local law for more than forty years.

Chief Peterson looked up at Tally. His face reflected a combination of curiosity and annoyance. It was nearly time for his dinner, and nothing upset him more than being late for a meal.

A television hanging in a corner of the dimly lit room was silently turned to *Oprah*. Harrison Ford was sitting next to the talk show host on a couch. Occasionally the chief glanced at the screen as if he were fearful of missing something important.

Tally looked around curiously. It was obvious that office redecoration had been done on a tight budget. It was dumpy, catering to the taste of the indifferent. Inexpensive pecan wall paneling and commercial grade green indoor-outdoor carpeting were the main decorations. Illumination came from a small desk lamp and two eight-foot fluorescent lights on the ceiling. An artificial ficus tree sat in the far corner, cobwebs stretching from the branches to the windowsill.

A computer station complete with printer and fax sat to the left on the chief's desk. The monitor was blank and the keyboard dusty. Tally wondered if Fred Peterson was computer literate.

A police scanner was positioned on a rusty and flimsy old typing table and occasionally crackled to life, scanner light blinking from channel to channel.

The chief's face was round and red from high blood pressure, and his suspicious hazel eyes grew amused as he examined Tally's ID. She guessed his height to be only about five-six and that he was well past the qualifying age for Medicare. His belly fell over the belt of his navy uniform, and his face was either scarred from a long-ago fire or a bad case of acne in his youth.

The air in the room smelled like nasty gym socks stuffed in a locker, and the floor hadn't been swept or mopped for months. Tally always figured how someone kept their office or home was a reflection on how they handled their job. In this case, she guessed Fred Peterson probably had a lot of untidy loose ends in his investigations.

Tally could feel his gaze move over her as he passed back her private detective license and settled back in his swivel chair. It was bulging and undersized for his stocky build.

Considering his bulk and age, he easily parked his left foot on the corner of his sturdy oak desk, the surface scarred with coffee cup rings, stains, and various scratches. Gingerly, and with a grunt, he raised his right foot, exposing a walking cast, and gently let it rest on his left leg. Tally moved quickly, grabbing a loose pillow from a chair sitting against the wall, and placed it carefully under the chief's leg. She smiled briefly.

"You didn't have to do that," he said, obviously unaccustomed to benevolence.

Tally felt a small tingle of sadness. She pegged Chief Peterson for a lonely, ineffective man. There was no ring on his left hand, and she wondered if he had a wife or children.

Eyes averted, he pushed an arrest report he had been reading to the side, lifted his wire-framed glasses atop his gray buzz cut, and asked with feigned patience, "What can I do for you ladies today?"

Rough-edged but far more wise than she wanted people to believe, Cid stepped forward, flashed her ID, and extended her hand. "Cameron. Cid Cameron." They inspected each other. She noticed his bony hand was frail and his fingers knotted from arthritis.

"Johanna Haskall," Cid continued, her smile becoming broader and more charming. "Whatever you can tell us about her death and investigation." She had learned long ago it was better to have other cops as allies rather than opponents. Cultivating friendships meant access to information that wasn't normally available to just anyone.

He looked up at her, enjoying the attention and respect she was giving him. His hands trembled a little as he tented his fingers. "That's an active police investigation. Not much I can tell you. Her family hire you?" He didn't wait for an answer. Just gave a what-the-hell shrug and rubbed his bulging stomach as if it were a child in need of comforting.

The chief pondered a moment, rolled a toothpick between his teeth. "I don't think about that case very often, not more than two or three times a day." His voice went cold. "First murder we've had in this area in over twenty years. Last one was a domestic dispute with a little of the wife's cutlery involved. The brutality of this killing shocked the hell outta me. And I don't mind telling you, freaked the whole damn town. Everyone is still jumpy as hell, scared to go out at night. Hard to believe anyone who lives here could be responsible for this kind of cruelty. Victim was tortured and mutilated. Haven't seen anything like it since I attended a course on sexual predators at the academy in Santa Rosa. Hell, when was that?" He seemed lost in memory for a moment and then shook his head.

"Haskall, what was left of her, was lying out there among

those beautiful . . ." He stopped short, the images flickering across his memory. "The wounds, the panic. She must have gone through hell." He shook his head.

Tally shivered, prickles running across the back of her neck. She could sense the fear and vulnerability of the women in this small, peaceful town. Johanna Haskall had been a pretty student without a care in the world. If this could happen to her, it could happen to them.

The chief continued in a haughty tone, choosing his words carefully. "Coupla months back, July sixth to be exact, I was on routine patrol and got a call at about eleven-thirty in the morning. Old guy from up the road and his wife were out for a Sunday drive and decided to give the flora and fauna a look before the tourists trampled everything. They stumbled across the body, out at Hughes Cove, shortly after they came into the clearing. Took 'em nearly an hour to walk back to their car and get to a phone. Old guy was hyperventilating when I got out there. Thought he was gonna have a heart attack and die for sure."

The chief looked up at Cid, studied her, and languidly smiled. "You retired badge?"

Pulling a dingy handkerchief out of her pocket, she dabbed her nose and wiped her forehead. The office was close and hot. Then she raised her hands in mock surrender, her blue eyes unreadable. "Thirty-two years. Lieutenant. Homicide. San Francisco."

He glanced at Tally. "And you?"

"Inspector. Homicide. San Francisco," she answered with a wan smile.

As she spoke, Tally noted the entire wall behind the desk was an array of commendations and photos of unknown dignitaries with the chief. Most were yellowed from age, all were dusty from neglect. The filing cabinet in the corner had stacks of paper on top as well as an array of folders beside it. Notes were taped to the side. Cartons stacked three high lined the only other wall.

Shifting in his chair, the chief accidentally nudged his injured foot. He turned another shade of unhealthy red before dryly muttering, "Shit. Damn bunions. Painful little bastards. Feels like that young sawbones cut half my foot off." The statement produced a deep frown.

"Feet are first to go, cop's favorite complaint," Cid affirmed, looking at her clumsy black orthopedic shoes. "I got great teeth, but lousy feet. Maybe if I'd poured a little scotch on my feet over the years they wouldn't be in such rough shape."

Still wincing, the chief scrutinized both women. The harsh lines etched around his mouth amplified his age and frailty. "So you want to snoop around the Haskall case, huh? Like I said, that's an active investigation. You understand?" He carefully pulled his feet from the desk and a little too politely added, "We all want to find the nasty bastard that killed Haskall, but that doesn't entitle you to inside information. You should know with your experience and your backgrounds the rules just don't allow for me to share much." He gave them both a contemptuous look.

"The rules are discretionary, as is your cooperation," Tally added tonelessly. Planting her hands on the back of a metal chair next to the desk, she found his arrogance an irritant and wondered if he was simply showing off. "And while you make up your mind what you're going to tell us, a killer and rapist is on the loose watching and waiting to kill again."

The chief looked her over from head to toe and rolled his eyes. "Cut the crap. This is my jurisdiction. I do what I please, when I please."

"Like contaminating the crime scene by moving Johanna Haskall's body?" Tally fired back.

There was a sudden flare in Chief Peterson's hazel eyes, and

28

beneath his air of pride and control, Tally perceived another feeling, perhaps incompetence. She had little tolerance for mediocrity, but she knew she was going to have to cultivate a certain trust with him if they were going to get anywhere.

She looked at his weathered face. "We're detectives, same as you. And we're all after the same thing. Peace for a grieving mother and the capture of a dangerous killer."

Cid felt a rush of irritation. She looked at Fred Peterson and their eyes locked. "This is serious shit. I don't like being jacked around. And I don't like the macho bullshit game. I understand everyone jockeys for a position of importance in a murder investigation, but politics are bullshit, and your unwillingness to help us out is not only insulting to us but also to your own integrity. Jesus, you got a stiff and no suspect in sight. Take our help."

The dark circles beneath his eyes deepened. He pulled the toothpick from his mouth. "Save your breath, I know the drill. I'm not some dumb-ass hick." His power play derailed, the chief searched through the papers on his desk, trying to save face. He scowled and pushed back, the wheels on his chair squeaking loudly.

He stiffened, hesitated a moment as if he were thinking quickly. He badly wanted and needed the solution to this case. Tapping the toothpick on his desk, he looked at Tally and Cid, trying to judge. "You're kinda nosy and pushy. But maybe that's not such a bad thing."

He took his time, pulled out a drawer and shoved a stapler inside, then looked up as if unfolding a conspiracy. "You didn't get any of this from me. You understand?"

Cid shot him a dubious look and sent him an air kiss. "We'll try and keep it out of the papers."

He gave a brief sardonic smile and with some effort stood, unsteady for a moment. "There was a time when an investigation was about cracking the case and putting the guilty behind

29

bars. 'Protect and serve,' they used to say. Nowadays I find myself spending more time dealing with cutthroat political wars. You know, local government wannabes and the top ranks of the sheriff's department . . . all anyone cares about is their ambition, career first. No one bothers to look where they're stepping in the process. Meanwhile, the victim is lost in the shuffle."

Peterson squared his shoulders and shrugged, white fluorescent light capturing his silhouette.

Tally and Cid looked at each other, catching the hurt in the older man's voice.

After an uncomfortable moment he said, "A homicide detail was assigned the case by the Coast County Sheriff's Department since there are no *official* homicide detectives here in Goldenrod. They worked out of an office about an hour farther up the coast. From what I understand it's not a top priority case anymore. Fucking spotlight isn't as bright as it once was. 'Cept for the folks here, the case has been forgotten by the public, and it never did hit the papers—least not the major ones. Big city people don't care what goes on beyond the boundaries of their municipality. Sheriff's office figures this was someone from out of town who just happened to choose Goldenrod as their dumping ground . . . and with the lack of evidence from the crime scene and the victim, they're sitting back on their haunches waiting for new evidence to fall into their laps. They've only got one investigator assigned to the case now, and he's a part-time boy on loan from another department up in Bradford County. Hate to say it, but I think there might be a little corruption in the sheriff's office. If it ain't that, it's damn poor leadership."

His tone was bitter, and his face sagged with defeat. "Not only is the sheriff's department ineffective, but I gotta mess here, too. Shit rolls downhill. One crime causes ten catastrophes. For over a month I've been in a power game with the Goldenrod Town Council. They're leaning heavily on me to resign my post. Younger blood, was how they put it. They got me by the balls. The fine hairs. They want a quick arrest and fast indictment. I either produce or I'm gone. There's nothing worse than blind power."

His voice now crisp, he edged forward, as if signaling he was about to say something of greater importance.

"My ass didn't get thin by sittin' on it. My jurisdiction is about a hundred and fifty miles square and I work it by myself. No deputies, no secretary. I know the drunks and who's cheating on their wife. Who's getting divorced and who's getting married. I know the gays and the lesbians. I'm here when babies arrive and when family dies."

A tic at the corner of his mouth spoke for the pressure and stress he was feeling. His eyes flashed. He slapped the edge of the desk, causing the tiny brass lamp in the corner to wobble and nearly tip over. His tone hardened. "These are my people. I was sworn to protect them. Until the preacher says 'ashes to ashes,' I have no intention of giving up my job.

"I don't mind telling you I didn't like stepping aside for those out-of-town boys." His voice quivered with emotion. "And I sure as hell don't like the way they handled their investigation."

Tally shot a dagger look at the chief. Fred Peterson was an open wound, and she just kept picking and picking. "But it was you who released the only suspect."

"You're talkin' about the spic? The little ferret?" The chief smiled with an air of superiority.

"Latino. Hispanic." Tally's tone was chilled as she took a step forward. The smirk on her face could not be mistaken for a smile.

He waved an age-spotted hand and uncomfortably shifted,

his lips white. "Bastard cried harassment. Said I was treading on his civil liberties. Practicing racial profiling, singling him out because he was Mexican."

Tally stood still, eyes wide open in distress. "And did you?"

Struggling for self-control, Chief Peterson gave Tally a fuck-you smile. "Hell no! He was suspicious." He jerked his thumb. "I found him hanging around Hughes Cove the day after we discovered the body. You know what they say about perps coming back to the scene of the crime. And the flaky son of a bitch didn't have a believable alibi for his whereabouts the day before." The chief cut a scathing look at Tally and Cid. "SOB laughed at me. Knew I didn't have enough to hold him." The admission seemed to drain the chief's anger.

Tally studied him. Took out her notebook. "You didn't have a choice. I'd have let him go, too." Her tone was vindicating, supportive, and it gained her points. "And the suspect's name?"

The chief's face looked drawn. He took a long, slow breath. She waited for him to cave.

"Thomas Garcia-Gonzales. And get this, a criminal justice major at San Jose State."

He randomly searched papers on his desk until he found a three-by-five Polaroid photograph. He pushed the snapshot across to Tally. A darkly handsome image stared back at her. He wore a leather bomber jacket, white T-shirt, and jeans and looked every bit like a male model. Wavy brown hair, cut short and neat. Soft gray-blue eyes that suggested a pleasant disposition and a sharp, chiseled nose that defined Thomas Garcia-Gonzales's good looks.

Cramming a cigarette in her mouth, Cid waited for the chief to object. When he didn't, she flicked her Bic and took a long pull. White smoke encircled the television and floated under the fluorescent lights. She watched Tally with a combination of pride and curiosity.

"Did the sheriff's department question this fellow?" Tally asked.

"Yes. They thought he was squeaky clean."

"But you interrogated him and thought differently?"

"Damn right." The chief's voice was firm now. "Still think there's something fishy. Cocky little shit with a swagger and eyes that don't miss a beat. Kind of guy who picks up women, fucks 'em, and walks away frustrated."

"Lot of us can identify with that feeling," Cid said, taking another pull on her cigarette and blowing smoke at the stained ceiling.

Tally was silent for a moment and then pushed a little harder. "Do you have interrogation notes I can see?"

"Notes?" the chief said with a confused laugh. He pointed at his head. "It's all up here."

Tally's annoyance showed before she could check it. She quickly changed the subject. "When you referred to the victim you said she was tortured and mutilated. Can you elaborate on that?"

Fred Peterson did not blink. "No. Talk to Doc. The medical examiner." A wall of silence suddenly went up. This confirmed for Tally what she had suspected from the beginning: neither the forensic team nor the sheriff's office had released all the information surrounding the death of Johanna Haskall. Dana had been given only what they wanted her to know. Something of importance was being held back.

"This Garcia-Gonzales, was he romantically involved with Johanna?"

"Far as I could tell, no. They was close friends. Like white on rice. But remember now, this boy wasn't real talkative. He's streetwise."

"How about drugs?"

The chief rubbed his gray stubble. "Not likely. Victim didn't need money. I would guess you figured out the mother's loaded, so no reason for the kid to deal drugs. And I don't figure her for a pothead."

"People can have two sides," Cid injected with authority, now leaning against the wall. "And everybody has their price."

For the first time, the chief seemed to regard the two women in his office with respect. He mulled Cid's statement for a moment but remained silent.

"And Garcia-Gonzales, is he a druggie?" Tally asked.

Fred Peterson shrugged. "I ran him. His sheet's clean. But that doesn't mean he ain't snorting or shooting up. He's got a sealed juvie record. Something about killing the neighbor's dog."

The volume on the television suddenly shot up when Chief Peterson steadied himself against his desk and accidentally hit the remote control. He quickly stabbed the power button, and the room went silent.

"Is Garcia-Gonzales from around here?"

The chief looked up into Tally's dark green eyes. "Born and raised in San Jose. Father owns a garlic farm in Gilroy. Mother lives in Santa Clara and works for the phone company. He's a good student, a bit of a loner, but well liked."

"What was the victim wearing? Did you find a wallet or anything?" Cid asked, flicking a half-inch ash in the metal trash can.

"Like I said, talk to Doc."

Again Tally sensed something unspoken.

"Anyone report Haskall's car at the cove? Or any other car, for that matter?" Cid pressed.

"Naw. That was tourist time. Lotta traffic on the highway. No one pays attention to a parked car. People stop all the time, stretch their legs, take a look at the ocean, drive on. At night, you got the kids carrying on in the backseat of their cars. We leave 'em alone."

A single bead of perspiration leaked through the chief's

stubble and rested just above his lip. He pointed at his foot and seemed to almost beg for understanding. "I'm laid up right now. Give me some references in Frisco and I'll check you out. See if your big-city expertise is worth a tinker's damn. If everything is satisfactory I'll feed you whatever information I have and anything useful that comes in, as long as you understand if you get lucky and catch this bastard, I get credit for the collar. Fair?" He blinked, his eyes burning from the smoke.

Cid was familiar with the sentiment behind the chief's voice. It was the same tone every crook used when they were backed in a corner.

As she stepped forward and leaned across the desk, Tally could feel the chief's raw nerve endings, smell his stale whiskey breath. This was a desperate man who had outlasted his power. He didn't move, but the gaze on his face was uncertain. She gave him a long, cool look. "You check us out."

The seagulls were squawking their song while off in the far distance fog was beginning to roll in across the water. For a moment they were comfortably silent, the routine of two old friends taking time to gather their thoughts. After a few minutes Cid asked, "So what's your take on old man Peterson? He get under your skin?"

The not-so-tactful remark was without judgment but made Tally feel judgmental. Pausing, she considered her words with care. "I'm certainly not in favor of age discrimination, but crappy cops give the good ones a bad name. He's bigoted, drifty, and over the hill and only wants us to see what he can control. And why is he so hush-hush about the crime scene?"

Cid looked at her and then gave a faint smile. "Don't sell him short." With considerable effort she stuffed her shirttail in her pants. "He's got cop's blood. A little old-fashioned. But it's home for him, Tal. What he knows best. And he's trying to prove to whoever will listen that he's still got the right stuff. He's a hunter and he doesn't want anyone telling him he's too old to look for his prey. He's just protecting his turf from the big boys." Cid stopped and hiked up her pants, exposing bare ankles. "I kinda like the old fart. Can't be easy for him being nudged out by a bunch of ingrates."

Tally grinned, pointing at Cid's feet. "You forget something this morning?"

Cid pulled one pant leg up, her thick, starkly white ankle glistening against her navy Dockers. "Mimi arrives from Seattle tomorrow. Had to clean the house and get the laundry done. Only have two pair of socks."

With a look of amusement, Tally shook her head, humor in her voice. "Clean clothes *and* a clean house. What a concept."

"It's been just me and my dog all these years, Tal. Never have given much energy to keeping house. You always said I was a little rough around the edges. And God knows I'm too old to change anything at this point. And I sure as hell am never gonna put on airs.

"Took me three Glenlivets just to get the house cleaned and another two to finish the ironing. Neat and clean could turn me into an alcoholic."

Cid's tone was pleasant but a little sad. "I've got a good heart, a few rolls around the middle, and my ass sank before the *Titanic*." She raised her head; her profile was filled with wonder. "I was a butterball before the turkey, and Mimi still wants me. At my age that's a blessing."

The statement, so distinctive in its acknowledgment of need, caused Tally to close her eyes.

"Can't believe she's really coming, even got the dog groomed." Cid's eyes crinkled at the corners, her gaze thoughtful. "Everything has felt so incomplete since I last saw her."

Cid spoke the words with emphasis, but Tally could see and

feel the loneliness, the hope. Two would-be lovers searching each other out.

The woman Cid had met two months earlier on a lesbian cruise, Mimi Wingate, was a computer programmer for Microsoft. She was not conventionally beautiful, with rich, nearly white bleached hair and a preference for exotic blue eye shadow, but Cid thought her glorious. She wore a halo of laughter and with Cid, shared a love of Glenlivet and moonlight strolls.

After just a few hours of conversation, Cid had the affectionate sense that she had known Mimi all her life and that each moment spent together was one of friendship and new discovery. She knew that beneath Mimi's humor and gentleness was someone honest and stable. She had even detected a measure of need. Following so many years of care and sacrifice for her now-deceased mother, Cid found Mimi's love a gift and her last shot at true happiness.

Somewhat awkwardly Cid smoothed her hair, her eyes thoughtful. "I want her to be happy here."

Tally was moved by the emotions she read in Cid's eyes. She looked at her without sentimentality and then on impulse brushed a kiss across Cid's cheek. "You'll both be fine."

Cid wiped her face as if Tally had left a smudge and with mortification waved her hand. "Jesus, Tal, don't get all emotional."

Tally regarded her in silence, so wanting to chase away the deep shadows of loneliness and allow Cid the same happiness she had found with Katie. Then her eyes focused on a seagull, watching the bird make wide loping circles. The air was warm and still.

"I need to call Harry, see if he'll clear the way for us to talk with the medical examiner up here."

Tally was referring to Harry Sinclaire, surrogate father and chief medical examiner for San Francisco County. He was a likable and lovable man whose friends and colleagues stretched far and wide.

Cid checked her watch. "We haven't got much time if you're gonna get back for your dinner date. Why don't you drop me by the sheriff's office, I'll nose around there while you check out the morgue?"

Tally nodded, pulled her cell phone from the pocket of her khakis, and punched in the familiar number to the San Francisco Hall of Justice. She waited while the receptionist paged the chief medical examiner from the autopsy theater.

Chapter Five
Wednesday, September 16
3:20 p.m.

A three-tier Gothic stone fountain bubbled fresh water just outside the entrance to the Coast County government offices. A half dozen social workers and a few technicians sat around the fountain smoking and enjoying the sea breeze that blew across the highway and down the brick walkway.

Their edges slightly shredded, an American flag and a California State flag fluttered and snapped in the wind. To the left, closer to the door, a sign announced:

Department of Health and Human Services
Medical Examiner's Office
Billie Storm, MD

The brown block building was two stories high with a reception area and security station. Since 9/11, handbags and briefcases were scoped and searched, and handheld metal detectors were used to scan each individual who attempted to enter the building. Appointments were mandated, and guests were allowed access to the building only after verbal clearance.

A picture of the movie-star governor hung on the wall just over the sign-in area, and a magazine rack and dark brown Naugahyde couch sat against one wall. A water cooler and several chairs hugged the other wall.

"Doc's office is down the hall a ways, maybe a hundred, hundred and twenty feet on the right. Ain't there, though. She's in the morgue working on pieces and parts." The young security guard cocked his head, chuckled impishly, and gave a silly smile.

When Tally didn't respond, he shrugged, cleared his throat and said, "You're lucky you caught her." His voice echoed off the bleak brown walls. "She's usually at the Bradford office on Wednesday."

The intercom buzzed, and a female voice cleared Tally for entrance. Opening the metal gate, the guard gave a mock salute and turned his attention back to the coffee machine on a counter behind his desk, pouring a cup.

Tally moved with purpose as she made her way down the blue-tiled corridor worn down by countless footsteps. Unlike the building that housed the morgue and medical examiner's office in San Francisco, the Coast County space was cramped and for the most part windowless. The odor on the other hand held the same distinctive stench of death.

She viewed the walls dimly. All blue metal doors were closed and each was labeled by function, such as Ballistics and X-ray. But for now, other thoughts were screaming at Tally's cop instincts. The more she thought, the more convinced she became that vital information had been held back from Dana Haskall. Her pace quickened.

Doctor Storm's office was located at the west end of the building with the double-door entry to the morgue just next door. A sign outside read:

STOP
WARNING
CONTAGIONS MAY BE PRESENT
RESTRICTED

Tally stopped, thought for a second, and pushed a bell signaling her arrival. She was immediately buzzed in.

The morgue was the same as the rest of the building—cookie-dough brown with a dull dark brown trim and blue tiles.

Partially covered by a green sheet, the body of a young man killed in an auto accident the night before lay on one of two stainless steel autopsy tables. A wood block under his neck braced his head to keep it from rolling. A microphone used for dictation purposes hung just above the corpse and to the right of a surgical lamp. A scale used for weighing organs was off to the left over the sink. The smell of stale blood and dried feces was overpowering. Tally cupped her hands over her nose and breathed through her mouth.

Doctor Billie Storm probed the victim's neck and face with a sponge, wiping blood and a few smudges of mud from the skin. Carefully, almost lovingly, she untangled dark ringlets of matted hair and pressed them into place with gloved fingers.

"The family is coming later this evening to ride with him to the funeral home. I don't want them to see anything that will make their loss any more painful than it already is."

She pulled the sheet over the head of the victim and neatly tucked in the corners before finally looking up and smiling. "Does this bother you?" she asked, pointing at the corpse.

Tally grinned, but her eyes were flat. "Dead bodies are easy, it's the living that scare me."

Rolling her eyes, the doctor smiled more broadly. "Tally McGinnis?" She adjusted her black square glasses, her voice conveying guarded curiosity. Lean, small, and bright-eyed, the medical examiner stood on a one-step stool next to the autopsy table. "Billie Storm."

Tally nodded. "Thank you for seeing me on such short notice."

"I haven't spoken with Harry Sinclaire in probably two years. It was lovely to hear from him and even nicer to learn he is considering retirement soon. Years ago, certainly more than I wish to count, Harry was one of the first men to support my appointment as chief medical examiner for Coast County."

Doctor Storm was a striking woman with incredibly smooth black skin and the bedside manner of a caring physician. Her features were blunt yet delicate and, as she did in college, she wore her hair in a short Afro and enjoyed bright magenta scrubs instead of the traditional blue or green worn by her assistants. The hollows beneath her eyes and a few wisps of gray in her hair were the only hint that she, too, was nearing retirement age. As Tally studied her, she found the doctor's smile warm and instantly wanted to know her better.

Doctor Storm turned to Tally with questioning eyes. "Harry mentioned you were a family friend and suggested you needed some help with one of our local cases, Johanna Haskall. Such a deplorable loss." She paused, removing her rubber gloves and tossing them in the trash.

"Harry didn't elaborate," she continued quietly, stepping off the stool and moving to the sink where she began scrubbing her tiny hands with a plastic brush and yellow disinfectant soap that smelled like iodine, "but he was more than generous with praise of you, Ms. McGinnis. He said you were trustworthy and honest and your instincts for investigation and crime resolution were nearly as powerful as your desire to touch people and make their lives better. Admirable."

"Please, call me Tally," she answered, slightly embarrassed.

The doctor nodded, pulled a blue towel from a stack next to the sink, and vigorously rubbed her hands. She flashed a warm smile and paused for effect. "He also said you were stubborn, had a need to correct the world's wrongs, and an even greater desire to resolve the misdeeds of the evil."

Tally's cheeks became pink. She met the doctor's smile with a half grimace. "Harry has always said I wasn't born, I arrived on the scene, and I didn't come out crying but inquisitive and a little rebellious. Love him as I do, he has a father's instinct to praise, protect, *and* control."

"Say no more." The doctor looked at her with simple tenderness. "We all should be so fortunate to have a friend like Harry." Nearly a head shorter than Tally's five-foot-nine, she paused, held out her hand, and warmly squeezed Tally's. "Now, bear with me, and I'll pull the Haskall file."

On a nearby surgical cart Tally noticed a particle laser used for detecting minute evidence, and on the floor, a Jack Daniel's whiskey bottle, half full, sealed in a glassine evidence bag. Two empty cans of Budweiser were also tagged and sealed in plastic. She looked at the covered corpse on the table and knew instantly drunk driving had been the culprit in the death.

"Twenty-year-old female," Doctor Storm began, placing a manila folder, a large brown envelope, and a plastic bag on the Formica counter. "Five feet tall, eighty-five pounds. I suspect she lost a good deal of weight while in captivity. There were also signs of dehydration."

Tally flipped open her notebook.

"When a body decomposes, water loss is common, but also there were no food particles in her stomach, and her digestive tract was nearly void of waste, suggesting she hadn't eaten for days." The doctor slipped on a white lab coat. Tally noticed her glasses were thick and that she squinted as she read her notes.

"There was dried bloody fluid around her nose and mouth.

Postmortem residue. Petechial hemorrhaging was present in both eyes. Cause of death was strangulation by ligature." She moved the plastic evidence bag closer. "A six-foot leather strap, handmade, with a slit at the end and numerous holes punched down the center. When the end of the strap is fed through the slit, a noose is formed."

Tally moved to the counter and pointed at the plastic bag. "May I?"

The doctor nodded.

She picked up the bag and examined the strap closely. It was thick and although neatly trimmed, appeared crude. Each hole, approximately an inch apart, was evenly cut in a circle about the size of a pea. The leather was dyed pale yellow, and there were wear marks around the holes similar to those seen in a well-worn belt.

Her stomach tightened into a fist as Tally began reconstructing. She winced at the thought of Johanna Haskall's pain and fear. To confirm her suspicions she looked at the doctor and asked, "What's your take on this?"

Moving gracefully, Doctor Storm took the bag from Tally. Her eyes were grave now, and she spoke softly. "I believe the victim was held captive and tortured. I found minute pieces of skin and wear marks on the strap, which suggest it was slipped around the neck, the end fed through the slit, and the strap was tethered to a nail or spike of some sort."

She pulled on a pair of latex gloves from a box on the counter and opened the bag. Using an empty jar she demonstrated her theory. When she tried an upward jerking motion the strap tightened around the jar. Tally could almost see Johanna Haskall struggling to breathe as the noose tightened.

"There was one deep grove on both wrists. This is consistent with someone being handcuffed or shackled over a long period of time. Probably a means of restraint when the perpetrator was not present. From the angle of the grooves it appears her arms were shackled above her head. She died in this position. Lividity, the blood settling in the lowest levels of the extremities, confirms this."

The doctor glanced at Tally. "Ligature marks, also on the victim's wrists, indicate she was bound multiple times. And there were several furrows in the flesh around her neck. Deep tissue injuries."

The doctor moved her hand in the air. "Picture a pegboard of sorts nailed parallel to the wall. Each peg approximately an inch apart."

She lifted the strap, holding it near her imagined pegboard. She was silent for a time, the scientist slowly fitting the puzzle pieces together.

"For whatever his reason, I believe the perpetrator moved the strap up and down the pegboard. The higher he went, the tighter the noose became, and the victim was unable to breathe. I can only surmise he drew pleasure from watching her suffer. He may have demanded sexual gratification from her, and when she didn't comply with his exact wishes or he was incapable of achieving an erection, he placed the strap over a higher peg, nearly suffocating her. Literally slowly hanging her."

Tally shook her head. "And this was done many times?" she asked, looking for offender traits.

"Yes, I am sorry to say. The abrasions blend together so I can't give an exact count. Her body had begun to heal in places, indicating torture took place over an extended period. Evidence suggests weeks. There were no defense wounds."

Tally thought of Johanna's lost talent. The symphonies and songs that would never be heard again. Compositions never written. Her roommate and friends who would mourn and miss her. Her mother left without a best friend. It was the little things that brought it home for Tally—and made murder personal.

"You mentioned sexual gratification. She *was* raped?"

45

"She was sexually abused many, many times. Foreign objects were forcefully placed in the vagina. I found wood splinters as well as various food particles. There was no sign of seminal fluid. Which means the perp either used a condom or was sexually dysfunctional, which is fairly common among sex offenders."

Tally felt whatever warmth was left inside of her slip away.

Placing the leather strap back in the plastic bag, Doctor Storm slowly zipped it shut, her silence deliberate, a signal of how deeply she felt for the victim.

Maintaining a few feet of distance, she placed her hands on her hips. Once more she smiled with warmth. "I have my medical degree, but I also have a PhD in criminal psychology. When I was younger, a fledgling pathologist, I found it difficult to comprehend human cruelty. Studying psychology gave me a broader perspective and a trace of understanding."

Her laugh was knowing. "It also gives me an excuse to chatter when I have a guest like you." Her tone retained irony. "You see, the dead aren't big conversationalists."

The confession was so candid Tally laughed. "I hope I'm more entertaining than a corpse."

"I can assure you of that." The doctor's smile didn't quite reach her eyes.

She was silent for a time. "Rape is about controlling women. Hate, anger, power, and pain. Johanna Haskall's killer demonstrated all the classic signs of a sex offender. This killer's rage could have been motivated by something the victim did to him, but I would guess this is a gender issue. He hates women, and I suspect because of the organization and lack of physical evidence associated with this murder, he's either done this before or studied forensic investigation. MO is learned behavior, and he seemed to know exactly what was needed for police to nail him."

Although aware women were more apt to use poison or knives when they killed, Tally asked in a low tone, "What makes you so sure this was a man who committed the murder? There isn't any semen."

The doctor removed her glasses and rubbed her eyes. Her stare was bleak. "Masculine power comes to mind. Most women don't have the upper body strength to strangle. There also were old bruise marks on Haskall's arms, suggesting large hands had executed the injuries. Even at five feet the victim would have been a feisty package for an average woman to catch and control, and women tend to be much less violent than men when externalizing their anger. But technically, at this time, there is no definitive proof this crime was committed by a male.

"There is a condition known as erotomania. An imagined belief that the victim and offender are romantically involved. Erotomania is often diagnosed in stalkers and sex offenders and is applicable to male or female. However, there is a feel about this victim, from the torture to her overall appearance. My strong sense is the perpetrator is male. Ever hear of a drug called flunitrazepan?"

Tally searched her memory. "The date-rape drug?"

"Yes. It showed up in Haskall's urine. Your perpetrator probably gave it to her. A means of keeping her dopey and under control. Probably at the time of her abduction as well as when she was in captivity."

Her jaw firmly set, the doctor stared off. "This is all supposition, but I suspect he's degenerating, becoming very cruel. Killing Haskall and raping her didn't satisfy him. He's become more sadistic. He kept her body for two months, disfiguring her, and he cut her hair off nearly to the scalp. By the angle of the cuts I would suspect it was cruelly done with a knife. There are areas where the hair was pulled out by the roots."

Tally's soft features rearranged themselves into a sensitive yet penetrating stare. "Hold on. This is new. No one, including you, has mentioned disfiguring before."

Summoning an image, Doctor Storm replaced her glasses and used her fingers to make quotation marks in the air. "The hidden clue withheld from the family as well as the press."

Grimly she continued. "Four patches of skin were removed from various areas of her body. All seven layers of derma. Murder is no longer enough for this killer. He has moved to the sadistic."

Mentally Tally winced. "Bite-mark eradication? Cannibalism?"

"No." The doctor watched Tally with anguish, the darkness in her eyes softened by the fluorescent lights. "Because of the intensity of the emotions involved, bite marks are normally deeper wounds. In this particular instance only the skin was removed. The surgery was performed postmortem with a certain level of skill."

Leaning her lower back against the Formica counter next to the sink, Tally slid her hands in the pockets of her khaki pants in an attempt to ward off the chill from the cool room. "A doctor? Surgeon?"

"I would think not. Someone with a working knowledge of anatomy. Perhaps a seasoned hunter familiar with skinning as well as some basic anatomy."

Moving across the room, Billie Storm pressed the button on a small stereo. The smooth, lyrical voice of Diana Krall suddenly filled the room.

Tally cocked her head, distractedly pushing her fingers through her bangs, more red than strawberry in the dim room. She grinned. "You're a jazz enthusiast?"

"Oh, yes. My daddy was the finest of saxophone players, and I used to play a mean clarinet." She gave Tally a reflective look, nearly giggling.

"He instilled a love of music in me that has been my saving grace nearly all my life." She flicked her hand in the air, the sorrow in her eyes reduced. "Music brings a certain levity to unavoidable sadness. I think he knew that and was disappointed when I chose medicine over music. But Mama died of influenza when I was twelve, and I had this need to cure the world's maladies."

Tally's green eyes conveyed curiosity. "Then why pathology, the medical examiner's office?"

For a long moment Doctor Storm was silent. She drifted away and then pulled herself back from some distant, unpleasant place. "In my time, especially being a woman, it was challenging to be accepted into medical school. To be a black woman attempting such an endeavor was nearly unheard of. Good internships and residencies were given to the top male students first, poor male students second, women third, and black women almost never. Hard as it may be to believe, I've always been a bit bullheaded." She flashed a brilliant smile. "Daddy used to say, 'Never stop until the song has ended.' Well my tune had just begun, and I wasn't about to give in to chauvinists or racists, so I took what was available and surprisingly found my surgical skill and unimaginable curiosity were a perfect fit with forensic medicine. I call it unwitting destiny."

Feeling Tally's empathy, Doctor Storm smiled, reached out, and touched her hand, squeezing the fingertips. "And you? What brought you to law enforcement?"

Tally took a step back, reflected. "My father. A brilliant attorney and champion of the underdog. He always believed if he did the right thing for people, everyone would benefit in the end. He taught me to get involved and to give back. After watching him in court for so many years, I loved the law but could never see myself as a lawyer. For me, investigation and crime resolution seemed a natural choice." Tally breathed deeply. As she turned to Doctor Storm she gave a lazy grin.

"And as Harry so eloquently told you earlier, I have my own stubborn streak, so owning the Phoenix Detective Agency and working for myself was another natural choice."

At this the doctor smiled slightly. They were silently enjoying the music. It seemed to make Billie Storm pensive.

"Daddy played at the Apollo in its heyday. In fact I was named after Billie Holiday. She was my godmother."

"I'm impressed."

Doctor Storm looked off in the distance, then reached out and touched Tally's arm. "Music is joy."

She waited another second and then rested her hands on the counter, fingers spread wide—she was the medical examiner again.

"This was not an impulse killing. In this case both the weather and a clever mind were at work. When a victim is left outside, weather can destroy some of the evidence. Which it did. But, with the exception of a small smudge of makeup, laser findings were also null. Everything was left clean and orderly. Prior to death, he had made her bathe. Postmortem, the body had been washed with bleach and other than a few cotton fibers found on Johanna Haskall's tongue, most likely from a gag, no hairs or other particles were evident."

"Makeup? Odd for a corpse, especially one that had been bathed."

Doctor Storm referred to her notes. "Smudge was found on the left shoulder. Minute, about the size of a fingernail. Brand name, Estee Lauder. Base. Rusted Roses was the color."

Using her right hand, the doctor pointed at her left fingers. "The tendons on the index and little finger were severed on both of the victim's hands."

Tally's eyebrow arched, a nonverbal sign that anger was bubbling deep within her. "She was a pianist. That would have destroyed her ability to play."

"Yes. Even if she had lived and the tendons had been re-attached she never would have played the piano again. Which led me to believe the killing was personal, and her fingers were maimed as an act of added hatred."

Briefly, Tally considered the notion that Johanna Haskall's killer had known her prior to abducting her.

Slowly, Tally shook her head, as if sorting something out, her voice dry. "Johanna was desperate and would have tried anything to gain sympathy from her abductor. She could have shared some of who she was, including the fact she was an accomplished pianist. She may even have offered to play for him."

Again Tally shook her head. "As much as I would like to narrow the field of suspects, this doesn't mean she knew her abductor in advance. She could have been trying to save her life."

"Sexual predators normally stalk their victims. They have a good sense of who they are long before they attack." As the doctor moved closer, Tally's eyes followed her. "One way or other he knew Johanna and her routine before he killed her. I am as certain of that as I am the cold hatred of this murder."

Tally liked this woman, liked her strength and her principles. Usually medical examiners were distant and cold. Doctor Storm oozed wisdom and knowledge.

She thought for a second, gazed up at the ceiling as if to reconstruct her thought process. "Did you find anything at all at the crime scene?"

The doctor stood straighter, her mind traveling back to the sandy bluff. "I am sure by now you are aware Hughes Cove was not the primary crime scene. Once again, weather was a factor. I suspect the body was disposed late, in the dark. The fog was heavy, accompanied by a light rain. Pools of water had gathered in the hollows of the victim's back. After measuring precipitation accumulation it is my guess the victim lay there for eight to ten hours. We do, however, have a compromised crime scene. Chief Peterson, in Goldenrod, did move the body, so my timeline could be way off. I also found blowfly larva, but I can't determine if that was produced at Hughes Cove or elsewhere. No pupa was found. Since it rained on the fourth, fifth, and sixth of July, the time frame is pure speculation and could be off by days. Also, because the crime scene was compromised, I doubt any evidence I have uncovered will be admissible in court. So essentially there is no evidence."

Doctor Storm paused, expelling a breath. Her expression grew hard. "Footprints were washed away."

Stepping into Tally's field of vision, she continued, "There are a couple of curious things that did turn up later." The doctor's voice held relentless patience. "She was on birth control, and the tox screen on her clothes came back positive for cocaine."

Tally's green eyes locked on the medical examiner. "So the perpetrator was feeding Johanna drugs?"

"No. It only takes three days for cocaine to clear the system. There was no evidence of drug use in her blood. Only on her clothes. The amounts were minute. If she was using it could have been weeks since she'd had a hit. Certainly prior to her abduction. But at the very least she probably was a recreational user."

"The dead have no secrets." Tally was quiet for a time as concern for Dana Haskall nipped at the edge of her mind. There was a mother-daughter story in there somewhere, and she couldn't help but feel the plot was filled with secrecy and pain.

"You said there were a couple of curious things that turned up. What was the other?"

For a long moment the doctor was silent, her smooth black

face a mask. She closed the manila folder and picked up the glassine bag. "This ligature is made of human flesh."

The hairs on the back of Tally's neck prickled. For a moment she allowed sorrow to own her.

"DNA confirms it came from a woman of Latin descent." A familiar blackness nagged at the doctor's heart. "The hide, if you will, was cured in urine. A process once or perhaps still practiced in Mexico and South America."

Reactively Tally drew back. It was her job to get information. Break down barriers. To flush out the truth. But even as seasoned as she was, the doctor's words were hard to absorb.

She shook her head, alarm clearly evident in her expression. "So an accurate assessment would be the perp *has* killed before?"

"It would appear so," the doctor answered thoughtfully. "A highly evolved serial killer. A fearless sociopath who accepts no blame for what he is doing."

"Why," Tally continued, the wheels turning, "would our killer leave the ligature at the crime scene?"

Slowly, almost reluctantly, the doctor turned to Tally. She spoke with cool precision. "The oddly perverted aren't necessarily logical. Their way of thinking doesn't line up with ours. For him this was his way to display his level of violence. He's proud of what he is doing and he wants everyone to know he is brutally clever. And he's probably baiting all of us. If he has killed before and gotten away with it, he's trying to test our skills. In an offhanded way, he's offering his help with the investigation."

Tally stared deeply as she toyed with the gold chain she wore around her neck. "Where exactly were the patches of skin located that were removed from the victim?"

The doctor's face was attentive. She took several seconds to check her notes. "Left shoulder. Left breast. Right buttock and just above the pubis." She pushed the brown envelope toward Tally. "This is a partial set of pictures. You may take them with you."

Tally opened the envelope and carefully studied each photo. Pain passed over her face. A moment's silence. "Was there anything else?" she asked, her cop antenna vibrating.

The doctor kept her voice even. "The body wasn't just dropped in a heap at Hughes Cove. The victim was strategically positioned. She lay prone. Her left arm stretched out to the side of her head, as if she were reaching for something. Her right arm resting back, running down her hip and leg. Again, there are pictures."

Tally regarded the doctor for a moment, caught between the visual image and the horrible indifference of the act. "And you gathered what from this?"

With a hint of puzzlement, the doctor shook her head. "No theory at this point."

Abruptly, Tally asked, "Nothing was found in the victim's car?"

Flipping a page in the folder, the doctor shook her head. "A couple of empty Pepsi cans. A McDonald's bag with a few very old French fries and three sheets of a classical music composition. With the exception of the victim's fingerprints and a few hairs, also the victim's, the car was clean."

"If the perp used Johanna's car to take her body to Hughes Cove, how did he get away?" Tally asked.

"I don't know." Billie Storm gave a small shrug. "That's your job to figure out, it's not my line of expertise, although he could have hitchhiked, I suppose."

"Or had an accomplice," Tally added, jotting a quick note.

Tally hesitated. Her expression went through several changes—puzzlement, deep thought, distress. "Why Goldenrod? Why dump a body in Goldenrod?"

Billie Storm felt her tension grow. "I don't know, but whatever the killer is thinking, I don't believe he randomly left Johanna Haskall here. There is a reason behind each of his movements."

As if sensing her thoughts, the doctor stood silently while a question formed in Tally's mind. "Dana Haskall stated Johanna had not been given a proper burial. Isn't it unusual for you to keep a corpse this long?"

A cart clattered in the outer hall. Someone yelled, "Jeez, Larry, be more careful." Tally looked at the double-door entry and then back.

Again Doctor Storm removed her glasses, pinching the bridge of her nose. She struggled for a tone of patience.

"The body was released to Kenneth Haskall, the victim's father, ten days after discovery." Her voice rose in dismay and then softened again. "Both Mr. and Mrs. Haskall signed the formal release. Now there is a violent storm of anger surrounding this issue. Mrs. Haskall isn't happy with the arrangements that he made, she wanted her daughter interred at her family plot in Menlo Park. From what I understand, a lot of legal wrangling is going on. She wants the body exhumed and moved. Until this issue is resolved, she considers her daughter not yet properly buried."

Billie Storm offered a tired smile, affection, and a glint of humor on her face. "Like I said earlier, having my PhD in psychology allows me only a trace of understanding."

Tally nodded with a knowing smile, closed her notebook, and slid it in the back pocket of her pants.

"Everything else is expert witness testimony. Such as tool marks on the ligature. Perpetrator's MO. Blood and gastric contents." The doctor picked up the evidence bag that contained the bottle of Jack Daniel's and placed it in a plastic container marked Serology.

"There is one other thing," she continued, placing a tray of dirty instruments in the sink. She paused, mouth compressed.

"This information was included in my report to the sheriff; however, I believe it was deemed insignificant. Which it well may be."

Tally sensed the doctor was picking her way through a jurisdictional minefield.

Her expression now keen, Billie Storm continued. "At Hughes Cove we cordoned off three hundred and fifty square feet around where the body was located. For three days we went over every inch of ground. Approximately fifty feet from where Johanna Haskall's body was discovered, some hair was found. This in itself is not unusual, however I found the circumstances suspect."

Her voice had a chilling undertone as she continued.

"The hair was resting under a bush, but not out of sight. It was as if someone had placed it there expecting us to find it. A perfect blond lock recently cut. Natural blond. No dye or bleach."

Standing straight, Tally folded her arms. "Go on."

Glancing at Tally, Doctor Storm regarded her with a measure of sensitivity. Her vivid memory was flawless. "It would not be unusual to find animal hair or even a tangle or two of human hair on the bluffs. But this lock was precisely cut and barely damp from the rain, suggesting it hadn't been there long. And it had been cut with a knife."

Tally mulled over what she had just heard. "And you think the perp left it?"

"I think it is a possibility. If he sees himself as superior to the investigative team, he's going to continue to offer help. That's classic sociopathic behavior. He's in control."

Tally walked across the room, stopped in front of a skeleton hanging from a chain, and slowly turned back, a sinking sensation in her stomach. "You think this is a message. A dispatch from the killer."

Their eyes met, and silent understanding rolled across the room.

Doctor Storm became still, alarm washing over her face. "I think this sociopath has another victim and is daring the police to find him before he kills again."

"But it's been over two months since—"

"You're right, and it's probably already too late." The doctor closed her eyes and let her head drop.

It was as if the silent gesture let Tally digest the truth.

Chapter Six
Wednesday, September 16
4:49 p.m.

A mongrel black dog darted across the street and sniffed Cid's leg as she piled into the BMW. Daylight was working its way to dusk, and the temperature had dropped from the upper eighties to the midsixties. The fog was heavy and moist.

"Been waiting thirty minutes, nearly froze my ass off." She swiped at the dampness on her shoulders. "Probably started to mildew."

"Good to see you, too, Cidney." A half-wounded glimmer flashed in Tally's eyes. She knew this was vintage Cid. Her caustic yet loving way of saying she had been worried about her. "I could shoot you, put you out of your misery."

"Shit." Cid flipped on the car heater and scowled, her teeth banging like castanets. "You'd think all this extra flab would keep me warm." She slapped her stomach. "Besides, I'm hungry as hell. I was thinking while I waited, if love was determined by the pound I'd be downright desirable." She checked the glove box. "You oughta keep some treats in here. Something full of carbs."

Laughter flickered behind Tally's eyes. Without answering she smiled, put the car in drive, and headed out to the highway.

They were silent for a time. Then they carefully debriefed each other. Tally first, then Cid.

"To some extent, Peterson was right." Cid folded her arms across her chest, feeling her cigarettes. "Sheriff's office isn't exactly corrupt, but there definitely are some big-time political games goin' on.

"About twenty years ago, after I made inspector, a fellow by the name of Sam Broderick was still in uniform. He was a total prick. Cocky, not full of ambition, and certainly not someone the captain viewed as promotion material. He stuck around San Francisco for two, three more years. Got married and then, at his wife's urging, took a job up here with the sheriff's department. Never heard from him again until today. Having family responsibilities must have agreed with him, kicked him in gear. He's under-sheriff. Fat like me and outta shape, but a pretty damn good cop. And he was eager to share information with an old compadre."

Cid shifted in the car seat and turned the heater down. "He says with the loss of jobs in the timber and fishing industry, the whole economy of this area is dependent on the tourist trade. No money flowing in, and these little towns will dry up and be taken over by urban sprawl and big-city governments. Gen X heaven."

Tally watched the recollection glisten in Cid's eyes.

"Apparently after Haskall's body was found, which, by the way, was peak tourist season, there was a lot of pressure and crap from the political machine to keep the case under wraps.

They didn't want those rubberneck dollars floating down the road. Lotta smoke and mirrors. Media info and coverage was kept to a minimum. The investigation was done quietly, and the final consensus out of the sheriff's office is the body was randomly dumped."

"And what do you think?" Tally asked.

Cid emitted a part grunt, part hiss and rolled up the sleeves on her white shirt. "Most people involved in this case are too busy making assumptions to listen to facts, so you know where the sheriff's department can stick their consensus. Anybody wants to dump a body, they do just that. Along a road, in the woods, or wherever the hell. But what they don't do is carry the victim a half a mile and strategically position the stiff. This was no dump job. The perp knew exactly what he was doing."

Cid's words seemed to distress Tally. She could feel her own confusion closing in. She didn't believe in coincidence and knew there was something obvious she was missing. "Why Goldenrod? There's something here. I can smell it."

"Damned if I know," Cid answered simply, but she, too, could feel the rumbling in her gut.

Changing the subject, Tally lifted her hand from the steering wheel. "The lack of media exposure probably pissed off the offender. Could make him reckless. Maybe even prone to mistakes."

Cid paused, blue eyes narrowing, as if sorting something out. "Meaning this wacko wants to see his misdeeds in print. If he doesn't, he's in your face. Gets caught in a frenzy and starts killing faster and faster."

In the distance a short way offshore, coming toward them to the right, a boat blew its horn. Tally seemed not to hear it. "Like Doctor Storm said, the killer is proud of what he has done. He not only wants recognition, but admiration as well. This isn't some lowlife with a double-digit IQ."

Passing a slow-moving white Mustang, Tally eased the BMW back into her lane and pressed down on the accelerator.

Cid braced her hands on the dashboard. "Jesus. Slow down. I don't like the prospect of getting mashed in a crash. Besides, I don't have any panties on."

Backing off the accelerator, Tally studied Cid, then her bare ankles. A little smile curled her lips. When she was truly amused, Tally's grin was genuine and infectious. "No underwear?"

"My mother always said, 'Wear clean panties in case of a car crash.' I guess she never considered laundry day."

Tally rolled her eyes. Then the cop in her again took over. Anxiety was boiling in her stomach. "What about Garcia-Gonzales, anything new there?"

"Clean. He has an alibi for the night the body was dumped." Cid took out a cigarette and held it in her mouth. She pressed on. "He was apparently visiting his mother in Santa Clara. Mom backed up his story. Coupla interesting things, though. Broderick says Garcia-Gonzales did indeed have a juvenile record. Had a little run-in with the neighbor's cat and dog. Set the cat on fire and amongst other things, cut the dog's balls off. Also had a thing going with Haskall. Claims they were in love and had been sleeping together for over a year. And marriage was a consideration, sooner than later."

This was the second time in a matter of hours that Tally had heard something that starkly contradicted Dana Haskall's version of who her daughter was. *Was Dana a duped mother or a clever liar?*

"That explains why Johanna was on birth control." She cut a glance at Cid. "Did you get an address for Garcia-Gonzales?"

Lighting her cigarette, Cid eyed the road through the flame of her lighter, then patted her breast pocket. "Yep. Mama Garcia-Gonzales and daddy-o Haskall, too."

Smoke slowly drifted from her nose. "According to Broderick, father Haskall is a loser. Regular shakedown artist. Hasn't got a pot to pee in and is in hock up his ass. Lives in San Jose. Gets a small government check for an old leg wound he got in Vietnam. Barely covers his rent. Likes his booze big-time and got to his ex-wife's pocketbook by milking his daughter for whatever he could get. Interestingly, in a moment of drunken enlightenment, he took out a million-dollar life insurance policy on Johanna six months before she disappeared, naming his humble self the beneficiary."

"Sounds like motive," Tally murmured.

The boat horn blew again. Louder and nearer.

"Greed at best and certainly not concern for his daughter's well-being." Cid's gaze was bleak. Her shoulders slumped. "If, by some chance, Daddy ain't the grim reaper, Kenneth Haskall gains big-time. For the mere token of his daughter's life, he'll be drinkin' Johnny Walker instead of rotgut and livin' in a deluxe condo on some beach, several hundred thousand jingling in his pocket."

"Hmmmm. And does Daddy have an alibi for the night in question?" Tally's eyes were steady as she glanced at Cid's profile.

"In the tank. The hoosegow. Cooling his heels." Cid pushed the button for the car window and flicked her ashes. "Arrested on drunk and disorderly. Didn't get out until noon July seventh."

"How clever and ironclad, too," Tally said in a languid attempt at humor.

Outside, the ocean and most of the coastline receded from view, lost in the fog. The small tugboat floated by, lights flashing. Night was closing in early. The temperature continued to drop. Cid stubbed out her cigarette in the ashtray and put up her window.

Suddenly Tally pulled off the road into an asphalt lot divided by parking spaces, past two green Dumpsters and down the drive-through lane for a mom-and-pop hamburger stand. The road was badly maintained, filled with holes and loose gravel.

An uneasy expression crossed her face. Instinct now guided her thoughts. "Suppose the timelines are wrong?"

"How so?" Cid asked, straining to see the large white menu board.

"We both know the crime-scene detective work was sloppy. The old folks found the body about ten-thirty in the morning on July sixth. Billie Storm's investigation suggests the body had been at Hughes Cove for eight to ten hours, but she couldn't be sure because Chief Peterson tainted the scene. We also know the cove isn't a huge tourist attraction. Meaning the body could have been out there since the fifth or even the fourth without discovery. Decomposition wasn't a factor because the victim had been dead for weeks. So Garcia-Gonzales and Kenneth Haskall's alibis could be worthless. If either one of them is capable of murder, then they're smart enough to construct an ironclad alibi."

The car was quiet, both women harboring their own thoughts, their own terrible torment.

Suddenly a small brown speaker blared. "May I take your order?"

Cid chose the deluxe hamburger special with extra mayonnaise and mustard, fries, onion rings, a large lemonade, and a slice of homemade pie. Tally ordered a bottle of water.

Pulling forward, her jaw set firmly, Tally rested her hands on the steering wheel. The killer's cruelty seemed more powerful. His presence tangible. "Doctor Storm thinks there may be another victim."

Cid's eyebrows shot up. "Where's the body?"

Their eyes met. "There isn't one yet. At least not in this jurisdiction." Tally's voice was filled with dread. "If this is a serial killer, and he's escalating, it's been over two months since he last struck. That's a long time for a psycho to wait for blood."

Fully focused, Tally dipped her head a little; her bangs fell into her eyes as she explained Doctor Storm's discovery.

"Now that's a hot tip. Lock of hair? Come on." Cid played with the idea, took out another cigarette. "I mean, jeez, Tal, don't you think if this scumbag was drooling for a game of cat and mouse he'd be straightforward? Lock of hair on an open bluff doesn't cut it for me. Damn seagull could have been building a nest and dropped it."

"And if you're wrong and another woman dies? Or is already dead?" Tally fired back, her face rigid with both challenge and impatience.

Sorrow for Johanna Haskall was pricking in her throat, and terror for another possible suffering victim pulled at her. She felt the physical ache deep in her heart, not just for Johanna but all victims of violence.

Instinctively, she looked at Cid, could see the concern pinching her features. Saw the worry wearing her down. Intent, she reached past her frustration. "I think he's testing. Watching. Listening. Savoring every move that has been made because of his actions. He kept Johanna alive for weeks. Maybe he's doing the same with his latest victim, gauging us to see who is smarter."

Lighting her Virginia Slim, Cid blew out a long stream of smoke and put the window down. She sank into her own thoughts. She knew the smallest detail, often first overlooked, could prove to be the one fact that ultimately solved a crime. And the possibility of saving another victim hung in her mind. Then their order arrived, and the tension of the moment evaporated.

The greasy aroma of cooked meat filled the car. Cid took two long drags on her cigarette, then squished the butt in the ashtray, tore open a small red-and-white package of salt, and sprinkled her fries before taking a bite of her hamburger and looking at it curiously. "Roadkill."

She took another bite, shrugged, and wiped her mouth with the back of her hand. "Okay, we assume the sly bastard planted the hair."

Tally pulled forward and parked the car in the lot under the arms of a large oak tree. In the field across the highway, two little boys chased a flock of seagulls that had settled in for the night. She looked at Cid. "The clues left at the scene are only those the killer intended to be found. Nobody knows better how to cover their tracks or contrive clues than a cop."

Shaken, Cid dropped her burger back in the bag, her appetite suddenly waning, the importance of what she was hearing growing in her mind. "Cop? Your point?"

"Fred Peterson said Garcia-Gonzales was a criminal justice major at San Jose State. He was the boyfriend. We need to check him out." She moved her sunglasses on top of her head.

Her expression a mix of interest and urgency, Cid reached in the backseat, grabbing the brown envelope Tally had brought from Doctor Storm's office. Silently, she spread the pictures across her knees.

"Death isn't ever attractive, but this is downright ugly." Johanna Haskall's bruised throat was a dark line, her lips nearly purple and parted as if gasping for breath, drool caked and crusted on her chin. Her skin transparent and bruised. Harsh reality cast in blood.

The crime lab team had been thorough. There were fifteen photos. The agony, Cid thought, of the victim's suffering in living color. "Bastard."

Her eyes deftly roamed the photos. "No defense wounds."

The statement reminded Tally, although she did not need it, of how vigilant Cid was when viewing a victim. She pushed her bangs off her forehead. "Nope. And no one is that timid when their life is threatened. It's a natural reaction to fight. Unless of course she knew the killer and felt safe with him." Tally's eyes were cold now. "Like if it were her boyfriend or father."

Cid stopped and seemed to warm to the idea. She plucked the addresses from her pocket. "Better call Katie, you're not gonna make your dinner date."

Tally started the BMW and drove out of the lot onto the highway, bottle of water clamped between her thighs. There was no traffic. It was as if life had stopped and was holding its breath waiting for news of the next grisly murder.

She had been working the case for a matter of hours and she felt she had stepped into a bloody, dark vortex full of secrets. The mystery, the killer, drew her in, but the thought of another victim ignited her determination. Pushing through the labyrinth, she pressed down on the accelerator. *The hell with no panties!*

Chapter Seven
Wednesday, September 16
7:22 p.m.

The moon walked across rooftops and hid between houses like the cream in an Oreo cookie. Cars hogged the curbside, devouring every inch of available parking space. A few students sauntered down the sidewalks and across well-worn dirt paths in the grassy areas, and thick, ancient oak trees hung over the streets, allowing only small spots of pink light from the street-lamps to touch the ground.

It was warmer in San Jose than it had been up the coast, still in the middle seventies. Voices drifted out of open windows, rising with debate or hooting with laughter, and then fell silent again.

In the darkness of night, Thomas Garcia-Gonzales's modest house had a sinister look. White paint, nearly gray from neglect, peeled and bubbled from the worn eaves and clapboard siding. Shutters that had once held the color of the sun had now faded to a milky margarine yellow. A tangle of grapevines climbed up the porch posts, and overgrown azalea shrubs hugged the house. The lawn was weedy but had recently been mowed.

Tally made a quick U-turn and pulled into a parking space as a white Jeep Grand Cherokee pulled out.

Face pinched, Cid finished the last of her lemonade. "Wild stuff, makes your asshole pucker. Mimi will like this."

Tally hid her smile, picked up her bottle of water, took a sip, and carefully replaced the lid. The focus of her eyes changed. "Johanna was abducted June tenth. Do we know what time of day?"

"After dark," Cid answered stonily. "According to Broderick, the roommate, Sissy or Carolina Childs, got home around ten. She found the lights on and the doors unlocked. Place hadn't been tossed. Haskall's dinner was on the table untouched. No sign of a struggle, so she must have invited her killer inside, or he took her by surprise before she had a chance to react. And her purse was on the table. Eighty bucks still in the wallet, so robbery wasn't the motive."

"If this is a crazy, he doesn't need a motive."

Tally's tone was flat. "What day of the week was the tenth?"

"Thursday."

Intent, Tally leaned forward. "Is Childs gone every Thursday evening?"

Cid was silent for a moment, brooding. A tall black man and a skinny white guy with knobby knees walked down the sidewalk, each dribbling a basketball. The comforting sounds of play.

"She has a class every Thursday until eight-thirty."

"So the killer knew Johanna would be alone. Just like Doctor Storm said, he stalked her and knew her routine."

"That would be my guess."

"Crime scene unit find anything?"

Cid hunched forward and opened the car door. "Only thing out of place was a long green thread found on the kitchen floor. Could have been tracked in by Haskall, Childs, or the killer. Common thread, Broderick said, type anyone uses for sewing. Could be a connection, pretty tenuous though."

In stark contrast to the outside of Thomas Garcia-Gonzales's house, the inside was resplendent. Maple wood floors varnished to a shiny gloss, accented by rich rugs that held an Aztec design. The gold upholstered couch formed an L to one side and was set off by three dark brown leather wing chairs. A smattering of wall paintings suggested both taste and prosperity. A half a dozen empty Miller Genuine Draft beer cans lined one windowsill, and three Swedish ivy plants dangling from brass hangers cast an almost feminine feel to the room. With the exception of the cans, the home was definitely not typical male college housing.

Barefoot, wearing jeans and a navy T-shirt embossed with the San Jose State Spartan mascot, Thomas Garcia-Gonzales closed his front door. "Sissy told me Mrs. Haskall had hired a private detective to look into Johanna's death. Retired San Francisco Police Department, she said. Regular kick-ass detectives." For a moment he seemed like a local neighborhood kid who had just met his superhero, his hands stiff, arms hanging at his sides, unsure of what to do next. Then he reached out, offered his hand. "I'm glad you're here."

From the description Chief Peterson had given, Tally expected to meet a darkly handsome, short weasel of a man. Instead she was confronted by a six-foot hulking mountain of muscle with the lean intensity of a fitness fanatic. His handshake, on the other hand, was weak, his fingers soft, fuzzy with black hair and almost wimpy. His voice was baritone, with deep resonance and void of accent. His face so smooth it was difficult to believe he shaved. He was gorgeous.

Garcia-Gonzales seemed to study her, and for a strange moment Tally thought he smiled at her, a hidden grin not meant for Cid's eyes. His hand rested on hers a little longer than necessary, and she saw there was a quality about the tension of his gray eyes that suggested something deep. All she had wanted was a quick first impression, she wasn't looking for anything threatening or suspicious, but instead of responding to his charm and comfortable home, Tally's skin crawled.

He took command immediately, pointing to the sofa. "Please have a seat." He sneezed, then snorted. "Sorry, I have bad allergies."

Taking out her notebook, Tally made a closer inspection of the room. Three oak bookcases lined one wall, and an old three-prong coatrack sat in the corner and held a trooper's gun belt, oiled and polished. There was no gun in the holster. The shelves were neat with books, magazines, and periodicals lying flat.

The kitchen was off to the side through a small alcove. A door to the right was shut and curiously bolted with a large hasp and padlock. Tally, puzzled, turned to Thomas. He avoided her questioning eyes.

She settled into the corner of the plush couch. Cid plopped into a wing chair, giving Garcia-Gonzales a look somewhere between curiosity and deep suspicion. "I understand you're a criminal justice major."

Garcia-Gonzales's eyes sparked. "Yes. I graduate in December. Then I'm off to the academy for three months"— he smiled, revealing perfectly straight white teeth—"and hopefully after that a bevy of job offers will pour in."

His gaze beamed down on Tally as if to impress her. He was wearing aftershave that smelled sickeningly strong and musky, and he moved closer to Tally as if physical nearness was a need. "Hope to join the FBI after I get a couple of years' experience under my belt. I'd like to be part of the team that nails Al Qaeda."

He stopped for a second and looked at Tally steadily. He seemed to weigh some hidden option, his voice choky. "With what's happened to Jo, maybe criminal investigation is a better choice. There's nothing I'd like more than to be left alone in a room with the bastard who hurt her."

The remark, although simple in its meaning, struck Tally as a clever way for Thomas to disclaim any involvement in the death of Johanna Haskall.

As if reading her thoughts, Garcia-Gonzales stepped behind Cid's chair. "I suppose you're here because you see me as a suspect. Given my race and the fact I was Jo's boyfriend propels me to the front of the suspect pack, doesn't it? I have nothing to hide. I am an innocent man."

Drawn by the anger she heard in his voice and the irony of his remark, Tally asked, "Race?"

In a voice sprinkled with palsy-walsy emotion, he went on. "Racial profiling." He pointed at Cid and Tally. "Everyone knows cops profile, especially white cops."

"We're here to gather information," Cid replied, "not play the race card."

"In that case let me set the record straight." He eased into a wing chair next to her, wearing the cunning, sly look of a suspect one step ahead of the law. "I didn't kill Jo. I was with my mother the night her body was dumped. I don't have a record, and I've never been in trouble. Not even a speeding ticket."

In a neutral tone Tally suggested, "Maybe that just means you're good at what you do. Stay one step ahead of the authorities. Strangling is an act of passion, and you were passionate about Johanna."

It was a sneak punch, and Thomas reacted before he could

check himself. "That's bull . . ." he stammered. His eyes met Tally's; they searched and uncomfortably penetrated. She wasn't intimidated. She was listening for what was not said, the secrets he was unwilling to give up.

Regaining his footing, he smugly propped his bare feet on a teak coffee table next to a stack of neatly piled *Better Homes and Gardens* magazines, cupping his flawless face with his left hand. His eyes were now moist, brimming. "I was raised Catholic. I believe in the Commandments. Thou shalt not kill."

Aching for a cigarette, Cid shifted in her seat. She looked around for a bowl of holy water to toss at Thomas, then scratched her cheek. "What was your relationship with Johanna?"

Shadows on the wall cast by recessed lighting wavered and danced to a silent tune as Thomas Garcia-Gonzales pulled his feet from the table, tucking them under his chair. It must have been the right question, because the darkness left his eyes. He leaned forward. "I loved Jo from the first moment I laid eyes on her." His head dropped. "We were planning a December wedding. We never fought. We both loved music, wanted kids, and wanted to spend the rest of our lives together. We talked about it hundreds of times. A quiet suburban life. It was perfect."

It appeared to Tally that Garcia-Gonzales didn't seem particularly worried about being a suspect or being questioned, and his grief somehow didn't feel real. Although there was a certain somberness about his last answer, he seemed to be enjoying the attention.

"And Mrs. Haskall, what did she think of your wedding plans?" Tally asked.

He stayed silent for a moment. "We didn't tell her. We didn't tell anyone. Of course, I wanted the blessings of the church, but we finally decided it was best to elope. Las Vegas."

"She doesn't like you?"

Garcia-Gonzales hesitated, flipped a palm back and forth,

sounding less certain. "I don't think it's so much me as it was the idea someone would interfere with her plan for Jo."

"And what was her plan?" Tally pushed.

"Worldwide concerts, recording contract. Marry a conductor, someone influential in the music business."

"But not a cop."

Thomas shook his head, his manner very sincere. "No. And she was pushing hard to separate us. She wanted Jo at Juilliard. Away from me. Away from San Jose. But Johanna was happy here in our nest." He sneezed and wiped his nose with the back of his hand.

"Mother-in-law 101." Tally said sympathetically.

He nodded.

"You told Chief Peterson up in Goldenrod that you weren't having a relationship with Johanna. 'Just friends,' I think you said." Tally frowned.

"I told the chief as little as possible. He treated me like dog shit. I have no respect for him. And he's a lousy cop. I could have taught him a few things."

"You're wrong, son," Cid said in a bantering tone. "He's ornery, probably suffers from irregularity, but he's a good cop."

Her attempt at humor was met by an ugly expression that silently told her she didn't know what she was talking about.

"Did you ever see a psychiatrist or psychologist?" Tally asked.

Thomas seemed to reflect, as if determining what damage his answer would reveal. "Once."

"That was money well spent," Cid added dryly.

His gray eyes darkened, and his face turned hard.

"Was Johanna seeing anyone else?" Cid pursued, quickly flipping subjects.

As if goosed by a loose spring, Thomas jumped to his feet. "Can I get you something to drink?"

Cid waved her hand, shook her head.

"No," Tally replied bluntly. "We need answers, Thomas, now."

Garcia-Gonzales sauntered into the kitchen without comment and quietly returned carrying a Coke. He stood next to his chair and looked at Cid. His eyelids rose slowly. "I said Jo and I were planning to be married. Why would she be seeing someone else?" The clipped sentence had the undertone of bravado, but his soothing voice seemed to be playing with them.

Eyes grainy from fatigue, Cid bent forward, arms resting on her knees. "We're grabbing at anything at this point. It's not unusual for someone about to get married to check out the dating scene, make sure they're making the right choice. Ready to settle down."

Tally and Cid became a unit, a practiced team of one mind determined to keep Thomas Garcia-Gonzales off balance. It was an old cop trick that they both knew well. They hit suspects from every angle with no logical sequence until they got the information they needed.

"If Johanna was seeing someone else, that's no reflection on you," Tally added, the voice of reason. "After all, you were Mr. Faithful. Played it straight and narrow. No cheating. Right?"

Thomas gave Tally a sidelong glance. The smile that followed seemed bitter and filled with arrogance.

Cid waited a second. She pushed herself forward to demonstrate her persistence and stared directly up into Thomas's face. She resumed talking, her voice conspiratorial as if quietly including him in their investigation. She wanted him to talk freely—and too much.

"Let's keep this friendly. We're on the same team. You're criminal justice. You know the ropes. Rules of evidence. Suspect's rights. If you saw something odd or out of place, you'd have been on it in a heartbeat. Right?"

Taking his seat, Thomas popped open his can of Coke. Tally

could see the wheels turning. If Garcia-Gonzales admitted Johanna had been seeing someone else, the admission would create motive. Jealousy. It also would show he had been watching and stalking her. On the other hand, he was a cop wannabe, and Cid's question had challenged his investigative capabilities. He wanted to shine, wanted to show how well he knew his job. His ego seemed to seesaw.

He caved. "Okay, when you're out on campus like I am, you hear things. My friends were looking out for me. Jo had lunch a few times with a bozo named Dent. Biker type. Scruffy beard. Bald. Lots of scars and tattoos." The turbulence of memory clouded his eyes. "Jo was elegant. What she saw in this greaser I'll never know."

Sensing something important left unsaid, Tally gave a look of mock sympathy. "That must have assaulted your masculinity. You and Johanna had a different set of values. She wasn't good enough for you."

Thomas sat back, speechless for a moment, then his voice went cold. "This isn't what I wanted. My mother was right. She told me to keep an eye on Jo."

Abruptly Tally stood, moved closer to Thomas, subtly crowding his space. She had him in a rhythm now. "Your mother is a bright woman, she must love you a great deal."

He looked past Tally and out the window as stars ducked behind clouds. Rain began to beat down on the sidewalk. He was desperately trying to get his thoughts in order. "My mother is very caring." His voice was throaty, almost sensual. He pointed to a picture on the wall. "Lovely, isn't she?"

From the style of clothing, Tally pegged the picture to be taken in the late sixties or early seventies, probably before Thomas was born. She was indeed beautiful, with strong features and long, flowing dark hair. She seemed self-possessed. Makeup and clothes perfect. Her eyes, though, were blank and betrayed no feeling. Strangely, she noted, there was no picture of Johanna Haskall in sight and no current pictures of Thomas's mother. On the whole, the room was impersonal.

"And your father?"

Thomas looked impatient and seemed to shrivel. "We're not close. I haven't seen him in years."

Instantly Tally felt an unsettling ping in her gut. She knew inside every killer was the stockpile of the past. She wondered if Thomas Garcia-Gonzales's youthful experiences and broken relationships with family were enough to damage him, to make him a serial killer. Shifting subjects, she asked, "Was Johanna sleeping with the biker?"

"No." He laughed, but anger showed in his eyes. "Jo was exquisitely beautiful, soft, and smelled of Shalimar." His voice was chilled, yet soothing. "No way she'd let him touch her. *We were in love*. Because she was raised in such an impervious environment, I think she got off being around weirdos. Sometimes I felt like she was just beginning to learn about the world outside of music."

Thomas took another sip of his Coke, Adam's apple bobbing. "I hear women in Dent's company have been known to disappear."

Warning or apprehension? Tally wondered. "Maybe he was her drug dealer. Maybe yours, too."

Cid jumped in, eyes flat and unfriendly. "Who's to say you didn't have a nose full of smack, flew into a jealous rage, and offed Johanna?"

"I don't do drugs," he shot back.

"Come on, Thomas. I may be an older woman, but I'm not an old dummy. Johanna had money, and I'll bet some of it went up your nose. Everybody does drugs in college." Cid put an edge to her voice.

Thomas tapped his chest. "Not this everybody."

"Maybe not, but Johanna did, and that would have made things mighty tough for you in the job market."

Again Cid and Tally flicked a nerve, surprising Thomas with their knowledge of Johanna Haskall's personal life. Tensing, he seemed detached from his surroundings for a second. No expression in his washed-gray eyes. He was silent, just staring at Tally.

"Feds are pretty intense when they do background checks. No cop job for Thomas, his wife is a druggie." Tally pushed, taking in every nuance, every breath of air. "And if you jilted Johanna, to get even, she might tell the investigative team you were a user."

He turned to Tally with a look so cool it sent shivers down her spine. "What difference does it make now? She's dead, so that's not my worry anymore, is it?"

"That's mighty loving of you, Thomas." Cid watched, saw something happen to his eyes again—a flare of vain fury. She had interrogated enough suspects in criminal cases to know the look usually meant they were calculating their own culpability.

There was a sudden, distant rapping sound from behind the padlocked door. Thomas became still then gave a dismissive shrug. "Neighbor's dog. I'm watching him for a few days. If I let him up here he gets on the furniture."

Tally raised an eyebrow but said nothing as she wandered over to the bookcase. Thomas's eyes followed. A new edition of Webster's dictionary sat boldly in the middle of a row of books, a Beanie Baby rabbit straddling the thick binding. She caressed a cobalt blue ceramic egg, swirled it between her fingers and then set it back down next to a tiny piano-shaped music box. The pad of her thumb skimmed a miniature crystal mouse. She was beginning to understand Thomas but was afraid she was missing the obvious.

She inspected the books and periodicals. Most of the books were standard criminology and police investigation text as were the periodicals. The selection of magazines seemed out of place. *Nursing Mother. Sewing and Quilt Making Made Simple. Wedding Planner.*

"Did Johanna spend much time here?"

His expression did not change. He nodded. "Yes." He set his Coke on the table, leaned back in his chair, and clasped his hands behind his head. "We spent as much time together as possible."

"What about the piano? Didn't Johanna need lots of practice time?"

"Mrs. Haskall thought so. Jo had different ideas."

Abruptly, Tally's voice became seductive. "You and Johanna have a good sex life?"

Barely audible, he whispered, "Bless me father for I have sinned," and then declared loudly, "Yes, we were great together." His gaze swept down over her.

She instantly felt violated and again unexpectedly changed the line of questioning. "Did you have other serious relationships over the years? You know, another woman you might have been engaged to?"

Quickly, Thomas shook his head. "I've had my share of women." He seemed to push out his chest. "No engagements. Because of my religion I knew I would only marry once." He crossed himself.

Cid nearly whispered, causing Thomas to lean forward. "Any of your other women go missing?"

He perched on the edge of his chair. "You're smooth, very smooth. And although I enjoy the interrogation lesson you're teaching me, I'm not going to be your punching bag." He started to get up.

Cid opened the brown envelope she had brought with her and dropped the pictures of Johanna Haskall on the table. "Here's another little tutorial for you. This was hate, Thomas, pure contempt, and we're not going to stop harassing you or any other suspect until we find the animal who did this."

He touched a finger to one of the photos and silently slid

back in his chair. Again his hand moved across his chest in the sign of the cross.

Tally searched Thomas's face and had the distinct impression she was watching a man without a conscience. "What you see there, the torture and mutilation, it's sick."

"I can handle being a suspect, but you're delusional if you think I'm involved. I know the truth. I live the truth." He stood, looking at Tally, hesitant, as if afraid of saying too much. "Check out this Dent. Rose's Tattoo Parlor."

"Oh, have no fear." Cid gave a thin smile. "We'll interrogate the asshole."

Thomas seemed to almost squirm with tension. "He's the bad guy."

Tally chuckled. "And if you kill women, Thomas, how bad does that make you?"

"Maybe you'd like a sample of my blood. That would vindicate me of any drug or rape charges." Ever the cooperative good boy, he flashed that grin again.

Cid made her tone mild. "Even though it's inadmissible in court, a lie detector test wouldn't be a bad idea either. Get everybody off your back."

He sat again, straighter. Cid thought she saw a slight flinch. She could sense the distress just below Thomas's fabricated calm.

Gentle, almost solemn, Thomas looked at Tally. "Killing is the easiest thing in the world. It's getting away with it that's hard." He smiled, as if the shock of his words brought him hidden joy.

To Tally, Thomas Garcia-Gonzales seemed a contradiction. One moment a little boy filled with hurt and misunderstanding, the next a loyal, inquisitive would-be cop bursting with integrity. He was insecure and neurotic. In Tally's experience, such people lied habitually.

"How many times have you been to Goldenrod?" Cid suddenly asked with undisguised dislike.

The question seemed to throw him, as it was supposed to. "Thomas?"

"Once. Just once." He shifted again, steeling himself. "The day after they found Jo." He ran his hand through his hair. Dark stains appeared under both of his armpits.

"And how about Johanna, did she go to Goldenrod often?"

"No. Not that I am aware of."

"Do you own a car?" Tally asked.

"Yes. A white Toyota Camry."

"How about siblings. You have any brothers or sisters?"

"No. I'm an only child."

"Hunt much?" Cid probed, looking at a stuffed mallard sitting on top of one of the bookcases.

As Thomas turned to Cid, there was something in his fine features that resembled pride. "Ducks and deer."

"Why would someone want to kill Johanna?" Tally asked quietly.

A faint note of scorn filled Garcia-Gonzales's voice. He shrugged. "Maybe to get even."

"For what?"

His body grew taut. "Jo was sweet and kind and to my knowledge never hurt anyone. She was like my mother in many ways, a saint." He paused, organizing his thoughts, and rocked a little in his chair like an infant being comforted. "But we all have our secrets, don't we. We've all got a past." A curtain came down.

Tally glanced at him sharply, struck by the coolness of his voice. His face, she thought, was impervious, like the chilled photo of his mother.

"How old are you, Thomas?" Cid asked.

"Twenty-four." His shoulders relaxed a little.

"And you've been in school how many years?"

"Four."

"That leaves a few years after high school unaccounted for."

"I bummed around Europe and Mexico. Traced my family heritage. Worked with people representing Cesar Chavez for a while."

Cid studied Thomas with smoldering eyes. Her voice dropped to a new low. "You kill dogs for fun? Skin 'em? Burn cats?"

His eyes flew open, dark with rage. His face grew blood red. "That record is sealed." His words were accompanied by a fine spray of saliva. "I was a kid. It's irrelevant to my life now and certainly has nothing to do with Jo's death."

"Whacking animals is psycho. I don't care how old you are. It sets a pattern for future misdeeds." Cid's voice was thick with confidence. "FBI is gonna look at your juvie record and turn their nose up at you. Local cops won't like it either. Like you said, we've all got a past."

His voice in turn held a warning. "You're full of shit."

"Sing your sweet tune, Thomas, but I'd lawyer up if I were you." Cid presented a sarcastic grin. "Inefficient Chief Peterson would like nothing better than to make one more arrest before he retires."

Thomas's lips parted, but no sound emerged. He seemed overcome with anger. "You're yanking my chain."

"When I yank your chain, you'll know it."

Chapter Eight
Wednesday, September 16
8:10 p.m.

The rain stopped and clouds quickly drifted east, leaving the night sky a sparkler of light.

Tally turned the BMW in at the driveway to campus security, a two-story structure near the center of campus. The fire department occupied the ground level, security the second floor. The building had been erected in 1966 and presented a series of tall, narrow windows with dozens of recessed fluorescent lights. The parking lot was half full, and a calico cat tiptoed along a brick planter in front, ignoring the car headlights.

Cid found the lieutenant in charge sitting at his desk. The nameplate over the pocket of his khaki shirt read Eugene

Bongiovanni. His uniform was spotless, and the creases in his pants were as sharp as the edge of the small pocket knife that lay on his desk. He rose to greet her, shaking her hand enthusiastically. A surprisingly young man for such a high rank, he was tall, lithely built with scant strands of thin brown hair brushed sideways to cover a bald spot at the top of his head. His tie was pulled down and his shirt was open at the collar, revealing the neck of a white T-shirt. He looked tired.

They exchanged the usual pleasantries—the weather, nice campus, the traffic. The lieutenant was watchful and curious.

"Long day. I'm surprised I caught you on duty," Cid began, sitting in a chrome chair with an orange plastic seat.

The lieutenant yawned, pulled at his tie. "Beginning of the school year is rough. Hundred calls a day from parents, all suffering from separation anxiety. Most can't find their kids and panic when they don't answer their cells. Kids are usually in class or partying, but Mom and Dad want us to track them down and make sure they're safe. Makes for some long hours. I'm always glad when October rolls around and things settle."

He leaned back in his swivel chair and ran his fingers across his narrow mustache. "My secretary tells me you're here about Johanna Haskall."

"Only if you've come up with something new since you talked with the sheriff in Coast County. Otherwise, I'm interested to learn if you've got any other students who have gone missing in the last couple of months."

In the haggard face of the young lieutenant Cid could see something troubling. "Not a student, an administrative assistant. Stella Fielding. Just turned twenty-one in May. Graduated a year ago. Some kind of degree in dance. Got through school working as a stripper. Used to brag about the amount of money she brought home from tips. She works downstairs in the fire department."

His voice was slightly muffled as he continued. "I know her

83

well, so I personally searched her apartment. For a young kid she has a nice home. Decent furniture, a few antiques, miniature crystal collection. There was nothing out of place that I could tell. No forced entry. She just didn't show up for work one day in July, and no one has seen her since. Car's missing, too. New VW Jetta. Green."

"You suspect foul play?" Cid asked.

Hands folded in front of his stomach, the lieutenant shrugged. "Stella's a little theatrical. Used to babysit for me and the wife. Seemed like a good kid, but she was kind of emotional and flighty. Her boyfriend said she's high maintenance. Needs attention all the time. He got tired of the drain and broke it off a week before she disappeared."

He shrugged again. "She could be a suicide, and the body just hasn't turned up, or she could be hiding out somewhere milking her disappearance for attention. Don't know. City police checked it out and came up with the same bucket of zeros. There's no family, but according to the ex-boyfriend, Stella has done the disappearing act before. Little problem with alcohol. He says she's a real rum ball. Goes south of the border for a few weeks, then drifts back as if she never left."

He was still. "Couple of things bother me. It's been two months now since she disappeared. If this is one of her games, I would have thought she'd be back by now. And her dog. A little white poodle. Mean, miserable bitch. Bit my ankle first time I entered the apartment. Neighbors got her now. But it never made sense to me, Stella leaving the dog. Even if she was going to kill herself, I figured she would have dropped off the dog at friends."

"Ever consider her for another Johanna Haskall?" Cid asked, trying to keep her judgment neutral. She took out her pack of Virginia Slims but did not remove a cigarette.

The lieutenant seemed to search for words, tapping his lips with his pen. "The thought crossed my mind."

"What does Stella Fielding look like?"

Eugene Bongiovanni stood, walked to the window, and looked outside, watching a few students on the sidewalk below. In the distant east, lightning cracked the sky. "Five-one, hundred pounds, dark blue eyes, and spectacular long blond hair. Not out of a bottle. Natural blond. A real hottie. And a big tease."

"A flirt."

Eyes averted, the lieutenant seemed to steady himself. "That and then some. Had a habit of letting her breasts graze my arm or back."

"She came on to you?"

"Yes, and everyone else. She's not stable. She wanted to know intimate things about my marriage. It got to the point I told my secretary not to let her in my office."

Cid raised an eyebrow. "Any other disappearances in, say, the last year or two?"

Eugene looked at her intently. He was as interested in carrying on this conversation as he was in the statesmanship of student government. "Nothing I'm alarmed about. Had one student just fly the coop. Brazilian gal, Indigo DeSantana. Another knockout. She was on scholarship with the swim team. Just disappeared. Left her clothes, the whole nine yards in her dorm. I got a call about two weeks later from her mother saying Indigo was home, pregnant, and wasn't coming back. Case closed."

"You do any follow-up?"

"No. This is just campus security. We're not set up for anything major. San Jose PD was satisfied she was knocked up and went home, so why shouldn't I be. I had her things packed and sent to Brazil, that's it."

"You said she was a looker. Give me a description."

"It's been a while. I think she was around five-three or four, black eyes, long black hair."

85

Cid's good cheer vanished. For the first time she felt in her mind the dark rumblings of killer traits and a definite victim profile taking shape. "Thomas Garcia-Gonzales, you familiar with him?"

He walked back to his desk, looked at Cid's cigarettes, and shook his head. "Sure, Thomas volunteers here. Nice kid. Type women like to mother. Full of charm. Smart as a whip, and he'll do just about anything for anyone. When he finishes at the academy I'd hire him in a flash. Why?"

"He's got a lousy track record so far: his girlfriend is dead, and he's got a spooky juvie file. You say he hangs around here. Maybe he has something to do with Stella Fielding's disappearance."

Glancing at Cid, the lieutenant absorbed what he had just heard. "Charge Thomas with youthful stupidity sometimes, but kidnapping or murder? No way. We do a security check on all of our volunteers. He came up clean. Good grades. Old man pays the bills. Up-and-coming star. Hell, I'd trust my kids or wife with him any day."

"I thought he was estranged from his papa?"

"That's what I understand, but he still gets a check every month. He's close to his mother. Talks about her all the time."

Cid's jaw line seemed to tighten. "Did Thomas know Stella?"

Eugene Bongiovanni dropped into his chair and heaved an uneasy sigh. "Yes. They were close friends. Thomas listens to everyone's problems."

There was a subtle shift in the tension between them. A new, intense awareness.

"How about this Indigo DeSantana?"

Picking up his pen, the lieutenant nervously tapped it on his desk. "Yeah. Thomas was broken up when she disappeared." He paused; his deep-set eyes were shadows. "He's the one who packed her stuff and mailed it to Brazil for me."

Cid's gaze grew pointed. "You've never talked to the DeSantana family since?"

"No reason." His voice was quieter now as comprehension unfolded. "I never considered foul—" He cut himself off.

She let the silence hang, pushed her chair back, and rose slowly, stuffing her Virginia Slims back in her pocket. "Medical examiner up in Coast County thinks the perp might have another victim." Cid paused for effect. "A natural blonde."

For an instant he was paralyzed. Finally, Lieutenant Bongiovanni whispered, "Jesus fucking Christ." He again was silent for a long time. "This is all supposition, right? Half-facts. Nothing you can prove or disprove at this point? I mean, this is a long ways from putting a noose in Thomas's hand. You've already labeled him a serial killer."

Cid leaned across the desk and spoke with assurance. "No labels, but the potential is there. So are the traits. Absent father, intelligent, single, white, egotistical. Hurts animals. Hell, in profile he's a classic psycho. And these victims weren't chosen by accident."

He watched her. "No pattern of deviant behavior."

"None we've found so far. You want certainty? Contact Brazil, make sure that call you got a while back came from DeSantana's mother and that the girl is alive and well."

Bongiovanni spread his hands, gave a small smile, his teeth big and yellow. "If I remember correctly Indigo came from a poor family. Mountain people. Not real savvy. I'm not sure they had a telephone."

Cid watched, waiting for her silence to work on him.

"I'll try. It'll take my secretary a while to dig up the file."

Cid looked at her watch. "My partner's with Carolina Childs at Johanna Haskall's old place. That's close by, right?"

He nodded. "Two blocks down. Elm Street. Second house on the left." His tone was distant, preoccupied.

Cid stepped around the chrome chair, fishing a cigarette out of her shirt pocket. "Be back in twenty minutes."

Sissy Childs and Johanna Haskall's house was richly furnished, catering to the good taste of the young women. For a somewhat modest neighborhood, the house was large and in impeccable shape. A huge marble fireplace was the centerpiece of the living room along with a Steinway baby grand piano. A white flowered couch with puffy pillows and two oversized armchairs filled the remaining space. Beautiful watercolors of flowers hung on the walls. Roses, poppies, pansies, and lilies, all in thin brass frames.

"Your artwork is gorgeous." Tally stepped closer as if the flowers had come to life and filled the room with their sweet fragrance.

"Why thank you. They actually belonged to Johanna." Sissy Childs gave a short shake of her head. "I would imagin' Miss Haskall will be pickin' them up soon."

Expression seemed to leave her pretty face. She was all big, round brown eyes that were filled with bright intelligence. Her face was framed by crisp shoulder-length red curls, with a complexion so freckled it was difficult to see her ivory skin. She was cute, Tally assessed, even with her hair flying in eight directions and her black sweatshirt two sizes too big.

"I miss her," Sissy whispered, her Southern drawl thick and warm. "We were best friends from the moment we met. More like sisters. We shared most all our secrets." Her slender frame looked drained of energy and much older than her years. "Part of me died with Johanna. I will miss her the rest of my life." Scraps of sadness surrounded her, and her voice was saturated with the pain of knowing that Johanna would grow no older. "If only I'd stayed home, cut my class." She fell quiet.

Tally listened to the *what if* confession, feeling the grief inside, the terrible weight of culpability that she understood all too well. She had always protected her mother. Kept her free from the refuse of her cases. And then while she was away on a cruise, an insidious perpetrator kidnapped and savagely beat her defenseless mother as revenge. The weight of that guilt squeezed and crushed Tally until she felt starved for air.

Ever so softly Tally said, "Johanna's death wasn't your fault. None of us can control bad people or their actions."

Sissy gave Tally a thoughtful look as she walked to the end table by the far side of the couch and switched on a white ceramic lamp. "We used to feel so safe." Sissy continued slowly, "Now I sleep with a twenty-two under my pillow."

Tally's expression was sympathetic. Instinctively she trusted Sissy Childs. "Why haven't you moved?"

"Johanna." She spread her arms with the air of her fine Southern lineage. "She's still alive here. Her laughter, the symphonies, her designer skills."

For a moment the room was quiet, filled with ghosts. Tally's eyes were large and warm. "You loved her."

Sissy flushed, faltered, but did not answer, allowing her head to drop.

Removing her notebook from her pocket, Tally changed the subject. "How was Johanna's relationship with her mother?"

Sissy looked at the piano, then walked to the middle of the room. Frustration clouded her eyes. "In some ways they were very close. They both shared a love of the arts. And they traveled all of Europe together." Restless, she moved to the fireplace and then turned back. "Miss Haskall is a very strong woman. I admire that, but when it came to Johanna, she didn't let her breathe. In the end, if you're wantin' a good huntin' dog you gotta set the puppies free to explore, to make mistakes, to learn. Miss Haskall just couldn't let go. And she wanted

Johanna to be a success at any cost. In today's lingo, she micro-managed her daughter like she was an employee in a large corporation, not someone to love. She foresaw Johanna's future, and her expectation was everyone else would fall into line with her plan."

Tally realized there was a painful honesty about Sissy Childs that only added to her credibility. "And what was Johanna's reaction to this dominance?"

"In her sweet way, she rebelled. She was careless and unsure of her direction for a while. Lost her virginity less than a year ago to some two-bit oboe player from City College, played hooky now and then, and tied one on most Saturday nights." Her movements became more fluid, slowly calming as she talked.

Sissy laughed, closed her eyes. "The ultimate rebellion—tattoos and belly button piercing. We decided about six months ago if we were to be truly independent women, a tattoo was in order."

She smiled, looking at Tally as if she were letting her in on a conspiracy. "I'm the daughter of a redneck watermelon farmer who believes tattoos are for sailors and big, rough marines. If he knew I had a little rose on my shoulder he'd bring his shotgun a-callin' lookin' for the weasel who defiled his daughter."

She raised her hand and touched her left shoulder. "I can't say Miss Haskall would have been much different than my Daddy. 'Specially considering Johanna showed unrestrained gluttony by indulgin' in four tattoos."

She walked across the room and curled up in one of the chairs, the cushions nearly swallowing her. "Johanna couldn't make up her mind between a rose, a butterfly, a heart, and a tiny bonbon. So she took them all. Two weeks of pain, but how she loved those tattoos."

An eerie feeling crept over Tally. She opened her notebook and flipped a couple of pages. "Let me guess. One on the left shoulder, left breast, right buttock and one just above the pubis."

Sissy looked at her more closely, sensing something left unsaid. She met Tally's gaze, spreading her hands in silent inquiry. When there was no response, a hint of humor crept back into her eyes. Surprised by her own willingness to be open, Sissy smiled. "Yes. The bonbon was etched in her pubic hairs." Her voice was animated. "She said it was a reminder of how sweet she tasted."

Sissy realized Tally was now close to smiling. "Those were big words for Johanna. Six months earlier she had trouble sayin' the word 'penis.'"

Tally gave a look somewhere between amusement and understanding. "What about drugs? Cocaine. Was that part of the rebellion, too?"

Sissy shifted uncomfortably. "I suppose. She was curious like any of us. She only tried it two or three times. She knew addiction ran in her family and was ever so fearful she would get hooked."

"How was her relationship with her father?"

"'Cept when he was drinkin', they were very close, she loved him. Idolized him. He's a regular guy. Down to earth and real. Her fame and fortune didn't matter to him, all he ever wanted was for her to be happy."

"But he used her, took her money."

"Don't know 'bout that. Somethin' you'd hafta ask him. I do know that over the last six months they got particularly close. There was somethin' goin' on with Mr. Haskall. Somethin' Johanna wouldn't share with me. She was real troubled. Many a night I heard her cryin' in her room."

"He come here often?"

"No. He didn't want to embarrass Johanna, and he doesn't have a driver's license. Made Johanna mad when he drove illegally. She'd usually meet him at a bar here in town. Sparky's."

"What do you know about Goldenrod?"

"Not a thing." She paused, then shuddered. "Never heard of the place until, you know, they found Johanna."

"So to your knowledge she never went there before?"

"No."

"What about Thomas Garcia-Gonzales?"

Suddenly, Sissy's dark eyes caught fire. "Major pain in the ass, y'hear?" She pointed at the flower paintings. "Johanna bought them all from him at a garage sale. He was like a stray cat after that, just kept hangin' 'round."

"I didn't realize he was an artist."

"Thomas an artist? He's not got the artistic talent of a snake. His mother painted those years ago. And the lineage of talent ended with her, I assure you. I read an article about her in an old alum magazine. She is a gifted woman—Olympic swimmer, dancer, musician, and accomplished artist. Thomas sold the pictures to Johanna just after they met. He wanted them back a short time later, but Johanna loved their beauty and didn't yield to his request."

Tally looked slightly puzzled. "If they were going to be married why did he want the pictures back?"

"Married?" Sissy jumped to her feet, her red curls bouncing around her face. "I reckon a statement like that is liable to bring Johanna straight back from the grave and marchin' through that there door." She tilted her head to one side, toward the front of the house, and then put her hand on Tally's arm, as if she had a need to touch. "Have a seat, Miss Tally, I believe y'all are in need of some Thomas educatin'."

She had Tally's full attention.

"He tell you they were gonna get married?" She sat in a chair across from Tally. Her voice had the sharp quality of someone who got to the point.

"In December."

"That's a hoot. They went out maybe three or four times. Johanna got to where she couldn't stand to be around him." Her words had an edge. "He had a thing for his mama that my daddy would say 'just weren't healthy.' He even wanted Johanna to wear some of his mother's clothes."

"You're sure?"

"Oh, yes. He'd come by almost every night and in her sweet way Johanna would tell him to get lost. You know, I have a test to study for. I need to practice the piano." There was a moment's pause. "More than once Johanna said she'd see Thomas following her around campus or bobbing behind some pillar when she got out of class. He called three or four times a day. And left presents or notes on the doorstep."

Obsessive personalities, Tally knew, felt they had the right to invade anyone's personal space. "They have a sex life?"

"No. She'd slept with her oboe player and a couple of other one-night stands before she met Thomas. She thought he was gorgeous, which he is, and at first she wanted to sleep with him, but she said he couldn't get it up." There was a sharp intake of breath. The memory of hurt lingered in Sissy's eyes. "He told her she had failed him. For days Johanna believed him. She was so naive."

"Did Johanna spend much time at Thomas's house?"

"No. I think she was only there for the garage sale."

Sissy looked at Tally closely. Her voice filled with more grief than accusation. "We didn't see him for a while, I guess it was early June, we'd already started summer classes, and he dropped by to tell her he wanted her to meet his mother."

Sissy shook her head, wanting to make sure Tally understood, a note of worry in her voice. "Now that I think about it, his visit was strange. It was as if he thought they'd never stopped seein' each other. You know, like they were really close. We'd been drinkin' some wine. A lotta wine. The alcohol was fortification for Johanna. She told Thomas to get lost. When he wouldn't leave she laughed at him and not too nicely suggested he go suck a Viagra. He never came back after that."

"To your knowledge."

Unnerved by the comment, Sissy merely shrugged.

"Thomas said he had recently talked with you."

"He calls every two or three days. Usually I let the answerin' machine pick up the call. I got careless this mornin', picked up the phone before I checked caller ID."

"The police said nothing was out of place or missing from the house. Is that correct?" Tally asked.

"That's what I told them, but I noticed a few weeks later when I was dustin' that one of Johanna's music boxes was missin'. A—"

"Tiny piano," Tally interrupted.

Sissy Childs shook her head. "You found it?" Her words were measured.

Tally nodded. "Did Jo wear makeup?"

"Johanna. Please call her Johanna. She hated Jo." She sat with her hands folded in front of her. "When Johanna dressed for a concert or some other special occasion, she always wore makeup. But day to day, never that I can remember."

"Do you know what product she used? The brand name?"

Sissy smiled faintly, shaking her head. "Sure. A cellist in the school orchestra sells Avon to supplement her income. She just barely gets by. Johanna felt sorry for her and bought a number of products including her makeup."

"And she wore Shalimar perfume."

Her face thoughtful again, Sissy shook her head. "No. Johanna didn't wear perfume." She folded her arms and sat a little straighter. "Did Thomas tell you these lies?"

With an air of calm she did not feel, Tally closed her notebook and put it in her pocket. "He definitely has fabricated a fantasy of sorts."

"Did he kill Johanna?"

"I don't know, but if I were you I'd keep my twenty-two cocked and ready."

Tally paused, looking at Sissy Childs. "What do you know about some fellow named Dent?"

Sissy was quickly on her feet. Her smile widened. "He's our infamous tattoo artist. Big teddy bear of a man. Sweet as molasses. Johanna thought he was the most remarkable man she had ever met."

"Did they date?"

"Heavens no." Sissy looked stoic. "It was that naive thing again. Johanna had never known anyone who rode a Harley and drank whiskey straight from the bottle. I think a part of her lived Dent's adventures vicariously. Whether his tales were true or not, she enjoyed listening. She so wanted to get in touch with who she really was." Sissy was silent for a time. "Dent was a burly big brother. Very protective of her. He even told Thomas to leave Johanna alone."

Tally seemed surprised. "How did Thomas react to that?"

"I wasn't there, I don't know."

"Does Dent have a first name?" Tally asked.

Frowning, Sissy shook her head. "Not that I know. Just Dent, and I think that came from an old motorcycle injury. He had a little hollow on his forehead."

"I can find him at Rose's Tattoo Parlor?"

Sitting again, Sissy shook her head. "No. I tried to reach him two or three times after they found Johanna. Finally one of his coworkers told me he didn't work there anymore."

Tally gave her a curious look. "He got fired?"

Sissy stared at Tally; her eyes flashed comprehension. "No. He just disappeared. Didn't even collect his last paycheck."

Oblivious to time, a gray squirrel nibbled on a few choice acorns at the edge of the road as Lieutenant Bongiovanni watched from his office window.

Far out to the right, in a small tree-filled park, only a spatter of pink security light touched the tree trunks. Tally looked at the squirrel as she followed Cid up the walkway, then turned back to the park. She did a slow scan of the shadows. There was no movement, and yet, she couldn't shake the feeling they were being watched.

Inside the building, the elevator door bore a new hand-printed sign: OUT OF ORDER. Cid grumbled as they walked up the single flight of stairs that led to campus security.

After introductions were made, Eugene Bongiovanni took a seat behind his desk, hands gripping the arms of his chair. Black stubble blended with the dark circles under his eyes. Cid noticed he somehow looked older than he had thirty minutes earlier.

"You had it right," he began in a clipped husky tone. "DeSantana never returned to her parents' home." As if by instinct, the lieutenant checked the 9mm at his waist. "I spoke with her older brother. He said the family got a letter from his sister about a year ago. She explained she had married, dropped out of school, and was moving to the Midwest with her new husband. They never heard from her again."

"Didn't they find that strange?" Tally asked, stepping to the window. She looked out over the parking lot and past it to the park. Nothing stirred. Still, the perception of an evil being watching tore at her, sending shivers down her back. Slowly, she allowed her eyes to follow the same path. This time she caught movement. A lone dark shadow stealthily moving through the trees. Stopping. Lurking. Waiting.

"The DeSantanas are a poor family. I had to call the village grocery store to talk with them. And the shopkeeper had to get the brother. He just called back." He continued slowly. "He said if his sister escaped the poverty he lives in, then the family was jubilant. He admitted, however, he had hoped Indigo would send money to him so others in the family could travel to the United States and perhaps find a good job."

Cid made a dismissive gesture. "Oh, she escaped the poverty all right, for a cold, lonely grave somewhere."

"Wouldn't they have expected Indigo to write or call?" Tally asked.

Bongiovanni's mustache twitched. "Don't know. They've got fourteen kids still at home, and the father picks coffee beans for a living. I'm sure they love their daughter, but one less kid to worry about was probably a relief."

"Was there anything out of order in her dorm room that you can remember?" Tally asked.

Bongiovanni stood and walked to the window next to Tally. He leaned there, palms flat on the sill, staring out. "I remember being struck by how poor she was," he finally answered. "She wasn't like the other kids. There were a couple of sweatsuits. Stuff the swim team issued and two, maybe three dresses. One thing that sticks in my memory was her ceramic egg collection. Wife collects eggs, so it sparked my interest. Naturally DeSantana's were South American. Beautiful, from what I can remember. Each one was a different shade of blue. From what I could tell it was the only thing she had from her country or village."

Tally looked startled, heard the clink, clink sound in her mind as the puzzle pieces began to fall into place.

Turning toward Tally, the lieutenant pulled his tie over his head and stepped back to his chair, looping it on the arm. "I remember something else. Can't for the life of me figure out why I didn't catch it earlier. The woman who called me, said she was Mrs. DeSantana, spoke perfect English. Not even a hint of an accent."

Tally leaned forward. "So you think the call was made locally by an anonymous female?"

His voice sounded naked, stripped of professional pride. "That would be my guess." He buried his face in his hands, then looked up clearly dismayed. Composure quickly regained, he gave them a calm, level look. "I called Thomas, but he didn't answer his phone. Left him a message." He picked up a Styrofoam cup of cold coffee and slowly swirled it as if it soothed him. "Told him no volunteering until the Haskall case was closed."

Tally watched the street. A solitary runner streaked past the building and vanished in the darkness of the park. She looked at the trees, then back at the lieutenant. "That's really going to piss him off."

Chapter Nine
Wednesday, September 16
9:26 p.m.

Alongside of Tally's BMW, only a white Chevy pickup and a maroon Honda Prelude remained in the parking lot. Clouds once again hung low in the night sky, casting a hazy darkness across the cars. Tally's cell screeched just as she and Cid stepped outside.

"Got ourselves another one."

Suddenly Tally's skin felt cold. The air around her was charged with electricity. "Where?"

Chief Fred Peterson's voice was a monotone. "Another pisser for the politicos. Same place as Haskall. Hughes Cove. Billie Storm's here now along with a coupla uniforms from the sheriff's department. Can't say there's much difference between the two bodies, 'cept this one's a blonde, and she ain't been dead long. Hair's been whacked off. Doc thinks she was offed late this morning. Victim's positioned the same. Another ligature around the neck. Doc also says there was more violence and abuse this time. He did a job on her. Pretty sadistic. Skin's missing on her ankle and butt. Bruises everywhere. Black pools. And she's cut up. Breasts are a mess."

"When was she found?" Tally looked at Cid.

"Coupla hours ago. About seven-thirty. One of the local boys out for a jog." The chief coughed and cleared his throat. "I figure you left out here about two-thirty. That means the perp was either watching you or showed up after you left. Either way he dropped and positioned her in broad daylight."

"He's getting bold." Tally felt herself squinting as she looked around the parking lot. Her hands were clenched. "And he's escalating."

"Doc said to let you know there was a smudge of lipstick on the victim's cheek. Sorta like someone had given her a kiss. Says she'll know more when she gets the body back to autopsy."

"Lipstick?" Tally asked, aware Cid was watching her.

"That's what she said." He grunted. "Green Volkswagen was left in the same spot as Haskall's car. Plates and registration are missin'. Got a trace on the vehicle VIN number, but probably won't get a hit until tomorrow. Everything's shut down for the night. Ain't got squat besides that. This bimbo is good."

"No footprints or tire tracks?" Tally asked.

"Nothin' I noticed when I first got here. See what Doc comes up with." Again Fred Peterson coughed, seemed to have trouble catching his breath. "Don't have a clue who she is. Even with her body in rough shape, I can tell she was a beauty."

Holding her breath, Tally was silent for a moment while a mental picture formed. "Your victim's name is Stella Fielding. Give campus security a call at San Jose State, Lieutenant Bongiovanni. He'll fill you in on Stella and her disappearance."

"Sounds like you've been busy," the chief said with a note of surprise in his voice.

Tally blew out a sigh. "Keep us informed. And by the way," she added dryly, "watch your back. Thomas Garcia-Gonzales doesn't like you."

"Hey, anytime that miserable bastard wants to cross my path, I'm ready for him. Show me hard evidence of his involvement in a homicide, and *he's* a dead man."

Instead of pushing her automatic lock release, Tally purposely walked around to the passenger side of the car and slid her key into the slot. She looked at Cid, felt a knot in her stomach she had not known was there. "Doctor Storm thinks she died this morning. MO is the same as Haskall."

Cid gave her a reflective look, the weight of another murder more than she wanted. Her head acknowledged the crime; her emotions and heart pulled back. Most cops got to the point where death couldn't affect them every time. If she had allowed that to happen, she would have been used up years ago. Her voice almost hesitant, she asked, "You think this new homicide is a by-product of our investigation and Garcia-Gonzales killed her?"

Tally shrugged, playing with the idea. "He knew Dana Haskall had hired us. Our involvement could have been just enough to ignite his compulsion. Remember, he hasn't killed for a while. He may have panicked, decided he had to kill her. And if he dumped Stella Fielding this afternoon he would have had plenty of time to get back to San Jose before we saw him." Her voice fell to a half whisper. "We're working on borrowed time. I'm afraid he may be escalating out of control. Hitting that frenzied area where one rape, one murder isn't enough to satisfy him."

"A binge murderer, where two or three women go missing at the same time," Cid added. "Damned bastard is like chlamydia or gonorrhea. Once you got it, you don't know how to get rid of it."

Tally nodded and smiled. "I want to check out his mother. See what she has to say. There was lipstick on the body."

Leaning against the car, she quickly filled Cid in on everything Sissy Childs and Chief Peterson had told her. She seemed distracted by her own thoughts. "Think about this. Mother Garcia-Gonzales has long black hair and she's a dancer, a swimmer, an artist, and a musician."

"So she's got talent, what's your point?" Cid dug a cigarette and lighter out of her pocket and lit up.

Tally's voice was calm, the rhythm of one sensible word following another. "Indigo DeSantana was a swimmer with long black hair. Stella Fielding was a dancer with long blond hair. Johanna Haskall was a musician with long black hair."

A slow whistle escaped Cid's lips. "His next victim will be an artist." A touch of concern crossed her face.

Glancing in her direction, Tally shook her head. "I don't think so. We're probably too late already. I'd be willing to bet in the last two years somewhere in this city an artist went missing and has never been heard from since." She watched her words register in Cid's eyes. "I don't believe it's coincidence that Thomas had a blue egg, a music box, and a crystal figurine on his bookshelf. I think they were trophies from his murderous escapades."

"Bongiovanni mentioned Fielding had a crystal collection." Cid opened the car door. "And the artist?"

"Along with the other little mementos there was a stuffed horse sitting on a dictionary."

"I don't like to put the knock on anyone, but what I can't figure out is why someone didn't pull these disappearances together by now." Cid's cigarette wagged in her mouth.

"No family," Tally answered, a sad edge to her voice. "Until

Dana Haskall came along, no one cared enough to push the authorities to find out what happened to these young women."

"We're taking the time to care," Cid answered quietly. "That's a good thing."

The wind blew across the parking lot, creating a miniature tornado of leaves and dust. Their silence had an unspoken understanding as the wind settled and the leaves softly fell to the hard pavement.

Tally furrowed her brow. "Doctor Storm said the ligature around Johanna's neck was made of human flesh. Someone of Latino descent. I would guess Indigo DeSantana was the mark. DNA would confirm."

For a moment the only sound was the buzz of the security light on the side of the building.

Tally collected her thoughts and raked her fingers through her hair. "Maybe this is too clean. Too easy."

"Meaning what?"

Something new crossed Tally's face, uncertainty and a trace of confusion. "Maybe Thomas is playing with us, just dangling bait to see our reaction. Or maybe he's covering for someone else. The real killer. There were trace amounts of lipstick and makeup on Stella Fielding and Johanna Haskall. Maybe our killer is a woman."

Cid took a long drag on her cigarette and exhaled through her nose, watching the doubt in Tally's eyes. "Back to the mother."

Eyebrows raised, Tally's face was now tense. She nodded. "Or maybe they're in this together."

Cid dropped to the car seat, slowly pulling her legs inside. Her chunky features had rearranged themselves into a pensive stare. "A Mommy and Tommy duo." She looked at Tally, blew a plume of blue smoke. "And Thomas says he's a man of religion. Let us pray."

As if to drive home her point, Tally asked, "What was the condition of Stella Fielding's apartment?"

"Bongiovanni says it was clean. No forced entry."

Tally breathed in again. "So, like Johanna, Stella felt safe with the perpetrator."

The strain of the day was showing in Tally's eyes. They were bloodshot and a little puffy, and frustration crept into her voice. "Why," she asked, not expecting an answer, "were the tattoos removed? And why Goldenrod? Hughes Cove specifically?"

She looked up at the cloudy sky as if an answer to her questions lay somewhere in the inky darkness and then back to the ebony park across the street. Ground fog slithered between the trees; the obscure form that lingered earlier was gone, replaced by a lone squirrel retreating to the safety of his nest somewhere in the shadows.

With few leads to go on, Tally knew she had to keep questioning, searching, hoping for the one clue that would lead to a connection to the killer. She stopped, checked her watch. "It's probably too late to call on Thomas's mother. Maybe we need to head back to San Francisco. Clear our heads and take a hard look at what we know. I could check on my mother." She lapsed into silence.

Cid patiently finished her cigarette, tossed it out the car door, and reached for Tally, letting her fingers rest on her arm. She looked at her with tangible tenderness. "Your mom is fine, Tal. Katie would call if there was any change."

She cleared her throat, trying to hide her emotions. "Let's tie up a few more loose ends tonight. I wanna take tomorrow off. Remember, Mimi arrives." She smiled. "Besides I need a drink. Maybe two. What's the name of that bar where old man Haskall hangs out?"

Silent for a second, Tally smiled. "Sparky's."

"Let's go."

Walking around the back of the car, Tally felt her keys slip from her hand. As she went down on one knee she heard the crackle of autumn leaves behind her. Then Thomas Garcia-Gonzales's muscled form emerged from the shadows. She was low and at a disadvantage, so she stayed put.

His index finger grazed her cheek. "You and your friend cost me my job tonight, maybe my career." A sly look crossed his face. "You both need to learn to mind your own business. You get my point?" He ruffled Tally's hair, playfully pulled at her earring. "Your hair is such a lovely color. It would be beautiful long. You should let it grow." He sneezed.

Suddenly Tally came up out of her crouch. A spinning kick caught Thomas in the ankle, dropping him to his knees. He sprawled forward, his face hitting the pavement hard. She grabbed his arm, wrenching it to his back, leaned to the side of his head inches from his ear, and whispered, "Don't mess with me. Don't ever touch me again, and don't threaten my friends."

Thomas jerked his arm free. "Mother of God." He gasped struggling to his feet, bracing his hands on the back of the car, his brain working quickly. "I'm not the enemy." He looked at her with loathing.

Cid stood by the side of the car door now, her hand resting on the .38 in the small of her back.

He stared at her, then back at Tally. "What would you do?" he asked, touching his chest. "It hurts in here. I'd rather have you shoot me than continue with this pain."

"Now there's a novel idea," Cid injected.

Suddenly he looked haunted. "We were looking forward to our future, and in a blink, Jo was gone. She's dead! Murdered! Now you and your friend"—he pointed at Cid, his hand trembling—"have told Lieutenant Bongiovanni some cock-and-bull story." His voice caught, then he whined, "This is an injustice. Stop punishing me for something I didn't do. I have rights. You can't do this."

"I'm not kissing your ass," Cid murmured under her breath, "I don't care how hard you pucker."

Feeling the tension in her shoulders, Tally blew out a breath, pushed her hair back. She heard Thomas's distress and wondered who he really was. A calculating man whose truthfulness she could not believe? Or an innocent victim? At times like this she knew she had to make herself cold and unmoved by a suspect's pain, but for the moment she was reminded of how much was riding on her judgment. How a suspect like Thomas could be ruined by one misplaced innuendo, one misguided allegation.

"Go home, Thomas, think about Indigo, Stella, and Johanna. Ask yourself about their rights."

The muscles in his jaw flexed. "I'm telling the truth." There was something spooky in his eyes, an arousal.

"Don't insult me," Tally fired back. "You wouldn't know the truth if it slapped you in the face. I suggest you spend some time smoothing out your seduction skills. The way we hear it, Johanna blew you off. And there weren't any marriage plans. You keep talking that kind of truth, and we'll nail your ass."

A measure of satisfaction passed across Thomas's face. "I'm not scared. Your mother is living proof or should I say half living proof you don't always catch the bad guy."

The painful comment grabbed Tally in the gut. She blew out a breath as the hurt settled on her shoulders.

He pressed on, his eyes dull, his mouth a sneer. "You see, you're not the only one capable of digging up and dishing out dirt. *Comme ci, comme ca.*"

A plane overhead dropped a howling sound around them, then slowly pulled away, leaving only the chirping of a few crickets.

Tally took a step back, eyes cold. "We must be making you nervous." The anger in her voice was barely controlled. "It's just not looking good for you, Thomas."

He laughed, his hand touching a small welt on his cheek. A deceptive calm surrounded him. "Maybe it's you and your friends that should be concerned. I'm just an innocent victim, you're the predator." He paused, his persona shifting from the persecuted victim to the sly inquisitor. His eyes were thin slits, nearly reptilian in appearance. "Are you scared?"

"Of this killer? Or you?" Tally's tone became flat. "Assuming the two are distinguishable."

Bitterness filled his voice. "The killer."

"No," Tally answered, recoiling. "He's weak. Stalks defenseless women. He hasn't the courage to face someone strong." She could almost feel Thomas's glare burrow into her.

"People are who they are." A moment's calculation. "Anyone ever come after you?" His voice was soothing but warning.

"You've got an attitude, Thomas, and if that's a threat, I said I'm not scared." Tally struggled for self-control.

How, she wondered, was she to reach this man and gather facts, without igniting the escalating animal?

He looked at Cid, held her eyes for a moment, and limped off into the shadows.

Chapter Ten
Wednesday, September 16
10:10 p.m.

The wide front door was covered with an array of paper and cardboard beer signs announcing everything from low carbs to zesty flavor. A neon Budweiser sign buzzed in the window, and in the bottom corner a hand-lettered red-and-white sign said the place was open Tuesday through Sunday, ten a.m. to two a.m.

Cid glanced around. There were five small tables in the back and a few high-sided booths that seated four and ran the length of one wall. A dozen bar stools upholstered in black vinyl were full. Rod Stewart groaned on the jukebox, and a wrestling match silently flickered on the television above the bar.

Locals bantering and laughing sat hunched over their drinks. A few swung around on their barstools and gave Cid and Tally the once-over. An old codger, his head clean shaven, nearly fell off his stool, then with the help of a middle-aged woman, her face wrinkled and rough, righted himself and resumed sipping his draft.

Two men who looked to be in their early twenties were playing pool across the room, with a young woman in tight shorts and a tank top that was two sizes too small hovering close by. She sipped a wine cooler and allowed her bleached blond hair to fall across her face, nearly hiding her eyes.

The bartender was older, with a few strands of lank brown hair combed across his bald palate. The badge on his white shirt read Rudy.

The light was dim and the air pungent with the smell of stale beer. Cid slid up to the service section of the bar and pushed a twenty across a small rubber mat.

"Glenlivet neat. Make it a double, Rudy, and a very dry vodka martini for my friend. Two olives."

He slid two napkins on a tiny tray, dumped the Scotch into a short glass, and waited for Cid to take a sip. "Okay?"

Cid nodded. "A fifth of this would do nicely." She took another large gulp and waited for the warmth to hit her stomach.

With the same precision he mixed the martini, filling the glass to the brim. "That'll be fifteen-fifty."

Cid slid another ten next to her twenty. "Kenneth Haskall. He here?"

Rudy watched one of the patrons climb down from his bar stool and head for the bathroom. He put his elbows on the edge of the bar and nodded at the end booth. "Likes to be left alone. Drinks by himself, talks to himself." He took the money. "Let me know when you're ready for another round."

As he scratched his head, Cid noticed Kenneth Haskall was another baldy, just like the bartender and several of the patrons. She looked at her drink and wondered if it was the alcohol or the pretzels everyone seemed to be pulverizing. She took a sip of scotch, touched the top of her head, and vowed not to eat the pretzels.

Razor thin, with a good two days of gray-black stubble, Kenneth Haskall sat slumped over the table. A dirty, heavily stained black Giants cap was pulled down on his head, the brim orange and crisscrossed with oily fingerprints. He was carelessly clad in faded Levi's and a red canvas jacket, both in need of washing.

Cid set her drink on the table. "Mind if we join you, Mr. Haskall?" She and Tally slid onto the worn wooden bench, not waiting for an answer.

He didn't say anything, but there was a sudden flare in his cloudy blue eyes. He lifted his glass of beer and drained it, slamming the empty to the table. "Who the hell are you?" His resonant deep bass voice held authority for a moment.

Nodding at the bartender, Cid motioned toward the empty glass.

"Private investigators looking into your daughter's death," Tally replied. Kenneth was older than Dana Haskall by a good five years, she noted. His fiftieth birthday had easily come and gone. And although he was dressed like a slob and unshaven, his nails were clean and filed, and the narrow rim of black hair that sprouted from under his cap was neatly trimmed. A businessman, Tally guessed, who had been brought to his knees by the rigors of life.

For a moment they were silent. Haskall was looking at her, staring. Burst veins were like crooked red roads in his eyes and made him look drowsy and transient. "Whaddya want with me?" He pushed the ball cap back on his head and leaned across the table, his beer breath odious and a pained expression on his face. "You're here about the exhumation aren't you?" His voice was indignant but not slurred.

"No." Tally twirled the olives in her drink. "We're trying to solve a murder. Trying to figure out who hurt Johanna."

"I'm sorry," he said with real regret. "I didn't know, I'm afraid I'm a little too drunk . . ."

Kenneth Haskall continued to stare at Tally, his face holding disbelief. "Thought I'd seen it all in Nam. There's nothing like identifying your dead kid." He belched. "I should be looking for her killer. And I should kill him."

Rudy delivered the beer. Tally pushed another twenty across the stained and notched table. "Keep them coming."

"Hang on, Rudy boy." This time Kenneth Haskall's words were spoken precisely, as if he were making an effort to sound sober. "If these fine ladies insist on buying, bring me something solid. Tanqueray on the rocks. Doubles." He smiled. His gnarled face had the look of hard use., bulging and swollen from alcohol abuse.

He wrapped his hands around the beer but made no move to drink. When he looked up there were tears in his eyes. "I can't believe she's gone."

A picture of Johanna Haskall's body flashed in Tally's mind. The violence of the crime seemed more powerful than the man sitting before her. "Tell us about her."

He scrubbed his stubble with the palms of his hands and sat back. For a second there was light in his eyes. "She was wonderful. From the time she could walk there was a zest about her." He leaned forward again, this time covering his mouth with his hand as if he were conscious of his breath. "She loved to fish. My little sophisticated musician could hook a worm and cast a line with the best of them."

He paused, lost in thought. "Her mother hire you?"

Cid nodded.

He picked up his glass and drank it down in one steady gulp. He slid the glass in Tally's direction. "I'd give that up in a second. Hell, I'd give up my life just to see Johanna one more time."

"Rumor has it she was supporting you." Cid's voice was a little cynical.

"Depends on how you look at it." He had the sense these two strangers didn't like him. He shrugged and watched Rudy cross the room with his drink. "I had a thriving clothing busi-

111

ness. Built it from the ground up and sold wholesale all over the world. When Johanna started high school, Dana joined me in the business. I needed someone stateside, someone I could trust to keep an eye on the whole operation. The pisser is I didn't know you couldn't trust family."

For a moment, he tried to remember his marriage and his business before it all fell apart. "Dana was good. My clients loved her, and the staff broke their butts to please her. She liked making the decisions. Running the show."

Tally watched, sensing how little fight this beaten man had left in him. He had come apart at the seams, and his only remaining virtues were his honest words spoken without prejudice. It made her sorry that she didn't know him under other circumstances, that she couldn't help him.

He spun the bill of his cap to the back of his head. "Then, like in real estate it was location, location, location. She was there handling the day-to-day operations, and I was gone drumming up business. Loyalties shifted. She paid staff bonuses I wasn't aware of. Literally buying their fidelity. She hated it when I came back from being on the road. Told anyone that would listen that I had poor character, was a crappy businessman. Our marriage became a joke. She wouldn't sleep with me, and she put Johanna in private school so I rarely saw her."

Kenneth's face changed. His voice turned hard. "About four years later, I'd just returned from Hong Kong and found a letter from the IRS waiting for me. I was two hundred thousand behind on my taxes. When I went to my accountant he told me there wasn't any money to pay the bill. He said Dana had been aware of the problem for months and that he suspected she had been skimming money out the business for years." He grabbed his glass and drank half the gin. "She took my daughter, my home, and my business. I sold off what was left, paid off the IRS, and have been drunk ever since.

"Memories blur. Pain becomes tolerable." He hesitated,

then added softly, "The sad thing is, doesn't matter how much of this crap I drink—it doesn't take away the fact she was right. My character stinks, I'm unsophisticated, and I was a lousy businessman. I trusted the wrong people, and it cost me everything."

To Tally, his words seemed a tragedy, as if he wished to reach back in time and change his life.

"That still doesn't explain Johanna supporting you," Cid said, sudden and sharp.

"Screw you." He laughed scornfully. "Her mother gave her money. Lots of it. What else do you do for your kid when you're a cold fish unable to show your emotions. Dana tried to buy Johanna's affections.

"Johanna kept whatever money she needed and passed the rest on to me. She figured her mother owed me. I didn't disagree."

Something seemed to break loose inside of Kenneth Haskall. "It wasn't the money or the business, you understand . . . Dana took my pride." He drained his drink, crushing an ice cube in his mouth.

"Vanity castration. She flaunted her success with the very people I had dealt with for years. I tried to borrow money to start over, but words like 'inept' and 'neglectful' followed me. Job interviews were disastrous. Eventually I faced the music, gave up, stopped looking for work. Instead of a gin lunch, I had a gin afternoon and then a gin night and finally a gin morning."

He stiffened, looked at Rudy, and waved his empty glass in the air. The lines at the corners of his eyes were deep.

He glanced at Cid. "So I guess the answer to your question is, yeah, my daughter supported her drunken old man. I have no shame."

Rudy pushed a hefty glass of liquid across the wooden surface. Kenneth pulled the drink to his side of the table, resting his hand on top of the glass as if to protect the gin. "When money is tight, I panhandle and drink beer." His words were starting to slur, the burst capillaries in his cheeks brighter. "Been doing a lot of that lately. This is a pleasant replacement."

"Dana didn't know Johanna was doing this? Giving you money?" Tally asked, realizing how caught in the middle his daughter must have felt.

He gnawed on a knuckle, wiped his mouth with the back of his hand, and belched again. "My ex-wife is a cold and calculating woman. She's accustomed to meeting in boardrooms and persuading the pricks inside to see things her way. She loved Johanna, but on her terms only. If she had the slightest indication about the cash, *she* would have killed Johanna herself." His words had the undertone of warning.

Tally felt surprise surge through her. "You can't be serious."

He shot her a fearless look. "Lady, I have an ax or two to grind with my ex-wife, but I assure you, when it comes to my daughter, my words are the literal truth."

"What about the million-dollar life insurance policy? Using your daughter for money came easy to you—how do we know killing her for even more money wasn't just as easy?"

Kenneth Haskall froze for a second, silent, appraising them both. The only sign that he had heard Tally was the darkness in his eyes. Slowly he picked up his drink and finished it in one long gulp. "Johanna is the only good thing I did in my life. Her talent came from my side of the family. My father was a conductor in Berlin, my mother a harpist for the philharmonic. Don't take what little pride I have left."

He scooted to the end of the table and with effort stood, grabbing onto the back of the booth to steady himself. He looked at Tally with bloodshot eyes. "Johanna flew all over the country. Hell, all over the world. It was nothing for her mother to whisk her away for a Saturday night concert in New York." He leaned back, nearly lost his balance. "After 9/11 she got scared. Thought some plane she was on might blow up. She gave me the money to buy the policy. She became the parent. Wanted me protected in the event something happened to her."

A tear ran down his cheek, catching in his stubble. "I forgot I even had the policy until the police asked if she was insured. I told you, when I need money, I panhandle."

His face had a deeper, wounded expression. "I signed the damned policy over to Stanford last week. AIDS research. You see, along with my other character flaws, I managed to stick my pecker in a few places it didn't belong."

"You're dying?" Tally inquired quietly.

"Yes."

"Johanna knew this?"

He nodded. "By choice I don't take the pills. I figure dying is something that just has to be done. Besides, the pills, they interfere with my drinking. Make me sick as shit. It bothered Johanna. Made her cry. She wanted me around as long as possible. Even with all my flaws she loved me." He smiled, and a sad vulnerability shone from behind his eyes. "She didn't understand her father is a coward. You see, I want to die, I just don't have the balls to shoot myself."

The startling answer hung there for a moment. Tally felt shame and pity as she watched Kenneth Haskall crumble.

He grunted and patiently said, "I've got maybe six months. If I had a choice of seeing my daughter or taking a million bucks, I'd pick Johanna hands down." He dwindled again. "Maybe, since life has been my hell, I'll get to heaven. See my Johanna again. Now, if you'll excuse me, I have to pee."

Chapter Eleven
Wednesday, September 16
10:52 p.m.

"I must teach you," he began, snapping the shackles around her wrists, "to obey. If you are quiet and do everything I tell you, you will live another day."

In the dim light, her pretty, petite face was as pale as if she were already dead, her hazel eyes darting to the door, then back to him. She had come to be tutored. He was to teach her the art of defense. Now, she was his. Her hands were shaking, causing the chains to clink, her long blue fingernails twitching in the air. She opened her mouth, but her scream was strangled by her terror. She tried to think, but there were no options. His face was there. His evil smile. His hands.

"Oh, sweet Jesus. Oh, God. Please," she whispered, her voice shaking, "let this be a nightmare."

He had chosen her from his list of would-be karate students. How stupid they were to trust him.

He touched her breast, pinched her nipple until she whimpered. His eyes roamed her shoulder-length brown hair. His fingers slowly, sickeningly traced tears that ran across her bruised cheeks.

"I'm so glad you dropped by to see me tonight." He could feel her tension and smiled. "I was lonely. Without you here my time would be empty. Stella left this morning. Actually *Francesca* strangled her just after breakfast. Toast with blueberry jam."

He wanted to kiss her. Wanted to touch her more. Wanted to see her bleed. He pushed back, allowed the song to enter his head.

Somebody loves me, I wonder who, I wonder who.

He looked around the room, breathed in the stench of death. He pointed at a dark form hanging from the ceiling in the corner. "That's another guest. You know each other. His name is Dent. He's been here a while. He is a treasure trove ready for cutting. He will finish my project."

"And this"—he opened the old refrigerator—"is Gertrude. Soon I will go on a picnic to the bay. A basket of goodies for the crabs."

She screamed, hopelessly thrashing her arms and legs.

He slammed his hand down on the table. "No screams," he said coldly.

Talking fast, his voice rose. "Francesca can be so ruthless and so demanding." He leaned closer, kissed the side of her neck. "I want us to become friends, spend a lot of time together. You must listen to me. You must obey. No screaming. No struggling."

He pulled a strip of duct tape and tore it from the roll. "I'm going to gag you. Francesca will be here soon. You see, she's waiting to meet you. She wants to make sure you measure up. Remember, you must be nice to her or she will hurt you."

Somebody loves me, I wonder who, I wonder who.

Chapter Twelve
Wednesday, September 16
10:52 p.m.

"We haven't got a damn thing to take to the cops. Nothing but the fact Thomas Garcia-Gonzales is a flaky son of a bitch and that his mother might be a dirtbag, too. The more we learn, the less we know." Cid finished off her Glenlivet and waved her empty glass at Rudy. "Everything is so friggin' complex. I'm afraid I may be missing something that's right under my nose. Maybe I'm getting too old for this business."

"No," Tally answered loyally, "the perps are getting darker."

Good detectives keep a tight leash on their emotions. Tally shouldn't have been feeling anything, but she was. From the bombed-out shell of a man that Kenneth Haskall had become, to the laughter and loyalty Sissy Childs displayed, Tally could almost touch the love these people had once felt for Johanna. Neither of them, she was sure, were butchers. Kenneth was too broken, Sissy too innocent. Dana Haskall had publicly destroyed Kenneth's ego. If there was any rage left in him, he surely would have taken it out on his ex-wife and not his beloved daughter. He was a weak man, a whiner, not a killer.

And why had Thomas shown up outside of campus security? It seemed so juvenile, so theatrical.

Tally shut her eyes, trying vainly to wish it all away. "I want to know what's behind the padlocked door at Thomas's house."

"And how do you plan on accomplishing that?" Cid asked, sipping a new drink.

Outside the window, rain fell and lightning still danced jagged lines in the eastern sky. Tally watched the fireworks with a tired fascination. "I'll ask him to open the door."

"And you think he'll just whip out his keys and oblige your request?" Cid asked, wagging a finger.

"If he's got nothing to hide, why not?"

"For starters, you insulted the hell out of him tonight. Besides, he's unpredictable, might be a little nuts, and I think he just wants us out of his hair."

Suddenly Tally was tired. Tired of tedious investigations. Tired of twisted personalities. She wanted to be home, in bed, with Katie beside her. She sighed wearily. "I don't think there was a dog behind the door. Dogs yelp and bark. The only sound I heard was bumping."

Cid put down her glass, assessing its contents. "You're thinking another victim?"

"I don't know what I'm thinking." Tally bit her lip. "He's guilty of something. I can feel it. And he's smooth and hard to read, but I also know he's not stable. His fantasies frighten me, and if he is the killer and he's escalating he could have snatched another victim before we arrived at his house."

119

"Guesswork," Cid replied sharply. "A lot of people act suspicious, but you can't tramp into their house and demand to know what's going on behind locked doors."

"Sometimes rules have to be bent."

"Very carefully," Cid said, finishing her drink. "Very carefully." She gave a snort and then a half laugh. "Remember the time Barney Hampton decided to play cop hero? Some drug dealer he had in his crosshairs."

Tally thought for a moment and then laughed. "He broke all the rules. No backup and no search warrant. Then he got his big tush caught in the bedroom window trying to surprise the supposed crack master."

Cid shook her head. "Who turned out to be a Girl Scout leader who had probably never taken an aspirin in her life, much less snorted or shot up." Her voice sounded more bewildered then accusatory. "Took Barney a few months to live that one down. Everyone in the precinct called him a *pane* in the ass, as in window *pane*."

Cid seemed to drift, her brain chewing on something important. When she did finally speak her voice was dry. "Why would Thomas be so bold now? Kill a victim and snatch another in the same day? Especially knowing we're hot on his ass." She glanced at Tally slowly twirling her glass on the bar.

"It's about his needs. His addiction. He has to keep killing to feel any satisfaction. Or maybe he's being told what to do," Tally answered firmly, glaring into Cid's blue eyes, eyes that had seen too much.

"His mother?"

With a sudden new clarity Tally shook her head. "Yes. She could be just as ruthless, just as addicted," she said, finally giving verbal credence to the thought. It sounded weak to her, yet it had a certain plausibility.

"You know, all the years I worked homicide I've seen husbands kill their wives, children kill their parents, wives stab their husbands, but I never understood what kind of mother kills." Cid's voice was soft, yet it suggested a deeper tension.

Tally apprised her, "Given the right circumstances, anyone is capable of anything."

A simple phrase, Cid thought, that held a deeper meaning. In a world gone nuts with violence, no one could be trusted.

"Haskall and Fielding weren't our murders. They didn't happen on our watch. If there's even the slightest chance I'm right, that there's another victim, I don't want the guilt of ignoring someone's silent cry for help. I don't want a body count on my conscience," Tally said.

Energy suddenly renewed, Cid slapped the edge of the bar. "I want this prick, and I don't care what time it is, we need to talk to his mother."

Tally bent forward, as if in private contemplation. She nodded. "First we stop at Thomas's house."

A night groundskeeper for a small apartment building was picking up trash around a blue Dumpster when Tally wheeled into a parking space a few blocks from Thomas Garcia-Gonzales's house. Across the street, a late night game of one-on-one was quietly wrapping up, the two participants walking wearily from the driveway into a dimly lit house heedless of anything.

The groundskeeper looked up and eyed Cid and Tally as they climbed out of the BMW, and then he quietly resumed his task.

It was still raining. Not hard, but steady. Most of the buildings and houses were dark as they passed, the occupants gone or asleep.

The walkway to Thomas's house was a black tunnel, the

front door shrouded in shadows. Tally and Cid waited until their eyes adjusted to the dark, their stance part edgy, part curiosity.

Cid moved to the open window, the lights were on in the living room, but there was no sign of movement.

The wind softly tussled Tally's hair. She resolutely knocked on the door, straining to hear and pressing her ear against the peeling paint. She knocked again, and then her fingertips lightly tried the knob. "Locked."

Belying her bulk, Cid eased noiselessly across the porch to the tiny carport. "Empty," she whispered.

Breathing rapidly, Tally peered through the open window. The room was without movement, the silence uncomfortable. She slipped her car key around the frame of the screen and gave a slight tug. The aluminum casement popped free of the molding, crashing to the cement porch with a loud slap. Tally caught her breath, waiting for Thomas to appear from some hidden spot inside. Her eyes narrowed, and she held her breath. There was no movement. No sound.

In the dark, Tally gave a faint smile of approval. "*Pane* in the ass, huh?" Palms flat, she hoisted herself up and quickly inside. Cid stood in the silence, unlit cigarette dangling from her mouth, eyes rapidly surveying the front yard and quiet street.

The house was as they had left it, neat and orderly, Thomas's Coke can still sitting on the coffee table.

Tally slid to the kitchen, back against the wall. She peered around the corner. Empty. She moved down the hall into the first bedroom. Empty. Suddenly, the angry barking of a dog broke the stillness. Fear grabbed her, and small beads of perspiration trickled down between her breasts. The sound of her steps seemed loud. She moved to the window and looked out. The neighbor stood outside next to his garage, a dog at his feet. She froze. The barking continued for a minute or two, then ended as quickly as it had begun. The neighbor disappeared back into his house.

She knew with every hesitation Thomas could appear from the darkness. Breathing harder, she was still, then made the same quiet inspection of the second bedroom. Nothing. Both bedrooms had been impersonal, defined by their coolness, almost as if no one lived there.

Moving faster, she went to the latched door and to her amazement found the hasp open and the padlock sitting on the nearby bookcase.

She looked back at the window, saw Cid watching her. Opening the door, she slid inside. She pressed against the wall, hoping to hold back the darkness and silently cursing herself for not bringing a flashlight. It took her a moment of sightless fumbling to find the wall switch.

Blinking in the light, Tally stood there, a steep cement staircase directly in front of her. Had she taken one more step she would have fallen blindly into a dark abyss.

She reached for her Glock, checked the fifteen-round magazine and pushed it back in place. With the gun cocked and loaded, she crouched, moving silently down the steep stairwell, fingertips lightly grazing the bare brick wall.

The fine hair rose up on the back of her neck and with it the anxious feeling of being watched. When she spun around, the staircase was empty.

Reaching the last step, Tally stood straight, allowing her eyes to slowly scan the cold room. A shudder of grief went through her, she staggered, as if she had been shot. A lone pair of shackles dangled from two cement-encased brass rings. A red blotch of dried blood stained the wall under each ring, and tiny strands of long brown hair were embedded in the rough brick between the two macabre bracelets.

She kept listening, trying to still her heavy breathing. Eyes opening wider, Tally stared at the far wall. A poster-size picture of Thomas's mother hung in the center, surrounded by pictures of six other women and two small girls. She recognized Johanna Haskall's face and knew without further explanation the other photos were of victims.

In a second, her senses sharpened, and her heart gave an intensified thump. Walking across the room, she slowly raised her hand to trace the silhouette of a black-haired child no older than six, with big innocent brown eyes.

From a distant place, in a voice weak with emotion Tally heard herself mumble, "Bless Thomas, Father, for he has sinned."

Chapter Thirteen
Wednesday, September 16
11:05 p.m.

"Don't deceive yourself, Thomas. The two detectives are like all the rest. They will reject you in the end. They will make you feel small and worthless. They will end up hurting you, taking away your freedom. You must do something."

The stench of violent death seemed to crawl up the walls.

Disregarding the ramblings, Thomas knelt before his latest prey, his hand moving slowly over the delicate creases of her skin. He imagined punishing her for not being more attentive. Taking her forcefully until she moaned with pleasure. His mouth touched hers.

"Thomas, are you listening to me?"

He stood, then walked to his sewing machine. "I'll take care of it, Mother."

Chapter Fourteen
Wednesday, September 16
11:23 p.m.

Her headlights cut through the darkness. "Focus on your job, focus." Tally kept repeating the words over and over in her head, but all she could see was the face of the black-haired child, and all she could hear were the little girl's imagined screams.

Cid sat beside her, conscious of the light traffic, yet her gaze turned inward as if she wasn't there. It was a gesture not of rejection but of deep thought.

Negotiating a lane change, Tally picked up her cell and punched in the number to her house.

"I would guess this to be Tally McGinnis calling so late," Katie answered in her sleepy Irish lilt.

Tally cut across two more lanes of traffic to turn right at the corner. At the sound of Katie's voice her pulse quickened, and she felt places inside grow warm. Her soft features seemed to relax. "We're going to be late."

"You're already late."

The remark, Tally sensed, carried an unspoken reprimand for missing their dinner date. Although she spoke in good humor, Katie had driven home her point. Some people spend their days trying to figure out how to get out of work, others live their job. Tally was the latter.

"I'm sorry. Things have really snowballed." Her voice was a combination of apology and concern. She told Katie most of what they knew about Thomas Garcia-Gonzales but stopped short of ghoulish details. She wasn't about to start lying to her now. Besides, Katie would know.

Katie took in a sharp breath. "I don't understand how someone could be so ruthless." Her voice bespoke despair. Whatever inner pleasure she was feeling suddenly seemed to evaporate. She was muted, a silent, uncertain rhythm of anguish.

The awkward silence allowed Tally to feel her own emotions—fatigue, confusion, pity, deep anger. She shook her head, changed the subject. "I woke you?"

"No. I was sitting brushing my hair. Naked, I might add." Katie teased coyly, her voice less strained.

"Hmmmm. The visual is enticing." Tally felt a familiar excitement, a flutter between her thighs. She could almost feel her fingers disappearing in Katie's hair. "Any calls?"

"Aye. There's a stack of messages on your desk at the office. Nothing of importance. A young woman, barely of high school age, did drop by to see you. She was full of pure blather, but very sincere. She thought someone of authority, a detective, might convince her mother that blue hair was the proper style of the day. She'd even managed to save fifty dollars to hire you."

Fascinated as well as amused, Tally laughed. "And you told her what?"

"I was quite serious. I told her it was your job to find the logic and connect all the links so issues could be resolved, but I included the fact you were deeply involved with another case and wouldn't be available for some time. And I did suggest she sit down with her mother and try and work out a compromise. Imagine a child seeking a detective in order to communicate with her family. There's so much we never say. Perhaps her mother will see her decision making in a different light after they speak. Big or small, every age has its own devil." She snickered. "I also added my detective was partial to purple hair, not blue."

"You didn't?"

"I did indeed. I told her I probably would soon be dyeing my own hair purple."

"I really think Kelly green would be more appropriate."

This time Katie laughed. "Then green it shall be, Tally McGinnis."

Pausing, Tally's voice dropped. "And Mother, how is she doing?"

A new excitement captured Katie's voice. "I stopped at the hospital on my way home. Your mother was looking well." Her voice changed. It was happier, softer. "The doctor dropped in during rounds and reported he believed that she was beginning to show signs of coming out of her coma. He said she could rapidly propel forward or remain in this semi-coma state."

Tally's voice caught in her throat.

"Aye Tal, when I held Victoria's hand she squeezed it. Not a strong squeeze, mind you, but enough to let you know fiery Victoria isn't going to settle for silence much longer."

Using a flashlight, Cid glanced at a map and silently signaled with her hand for Tally to make a turn.

Tally looked out the window, cranking the wheel sharply to

128

the left. Her face was less tight, the creases at the corners of her eyes less deep. Her mind drifted, and she thought about what her life would be like without Katie's warm presence. She shivered, pushing the phone closer to her cheek. Her voice was soft, but clear. "Thank you."

Katie could feel the weight lift from Tally and for now, chose to let Tally digest what she had told her without further comment.

"Oh. And a call came to your mother's room while I was there. It was a wee bit strange as the man seemed more interested in you than Victoria. A fellow by the name of Steven Chandler. A reporter for the *San Jose Mercury*."

Katie continued, "I felt sorry for him, he kept sneezing between questions. A cold or allergies I would imagine. He was almost over-solicitous. He wanted to know where you lived so he could interview you."

Tally felt the car close in on her as she reflected on her own stupidity. She should have known Thomas would probe into her personal life. She chided herself for how much this case, all the cases, had endangered Katie. "And you told him what?"

"Only what the *Chronicle* had already reported. How Victoria was injured." She went through everything fact by fact.

A collage of Thomas Garcia-Gonzales's facial expressions flashed in Tally's mind. Conning sneers, innocent crooked grin, empty, fearless eyes. Was the call a threat to Katie or a warning to Tally? "Did he ask anything else?"

Katie could hear the alarm. "He flirted some. Got around to asking me what I looked like. I told him I was your partner and wasn't interested in his shenanigans."

"Did he ask you if you had long hair?"

Silence. "Yes."

"And you answered?"

"Yes. What's this all about, Tal?"

Anger and fear ran through Tally. "Just keep the door

locked, and don't go out. And Katie, my thirty-eight is in the dresser drawer, get it and keep it with you."

Katie shut her eyes. "And you'll be home soon?"

"As quickly as possible. I can't wait to see that green hair."

Framed by the moonlight and clouds, the hills surrounding Santa Clara were standing sentinel over the city. In daylight, the hot sun had baked the rolling tundra to a rich caramel brown. At night, the knobby ridges were silent shadowy ghosts, pimpled by an occasional streetlamp.

The Garcia-Gonzales house was one of three sprawling ranch-style masterpieces set into the hillside. The color of the outside of the roomy home was indistinguishable in the darkness. The landscaping looked as though it was professionally cared for, and a small cedar deck bathed in street light was an obstacle course of elegantly furnished black wrought iron table and chairs.

Tally knocked on the door and then rang the bell. In the distance a car alarm went off, sending an annoying burst of beeps across the rolling hills. It was difficult to determine where the sound originated, but Tally was sure it was coming from several blocks away.

"Only thing those damn alarms are good for is to wake you up in the middle of the night. Kids want your car, they're gonna steal it. Alarm or no alarm." The racket finally gave way to the sounds of nature.

Cid shifted her feet and checked her watch. "Less than twelve hours, and Mimi will be here."

Tally smiled, saw the excitement, but said nothing.

They waited, knocked again. Crickets played a symphony, and the last seasonal gathering of mosquitoes behaved like drunken pilots on a kamikaze mission, buzzing around Cid and Tally.

There was a stirring, then a rattle. Lights flickered on. First inside, then high-pressure sodium beams illuminated the front yard and driveway creating a series of gleaming shadows. The grass and tall oak trees turned pink in the glare.

A single bulb illuminated the rough cedar entry. "Who is it?" someone called from behind the glass-paneled front door.

Tally and Cid identified themselves.

Someone peered at them. "My goodness, it's nearly midnight." She paused. "I'm sorry, but I don't open my doors to strangers. If you need help I'll call the police for you."

The voice behind the words seemed out of place. Different somehow from what Tally had expected. Older perhaps, more reserved, but not cunning or conspiratorial.

"I'm sorry about the hour, and no, we don't need the police." Tally paused, her words bouncing off the front door like raindrops on the pavement. "We have a few questions about your son and Johanna Haskall. It's urgent we get answers right away. Do you mind if we speak to you from out here?"

She pondered that for a moment. "It's late. Can't it wait until tomorrow? Besides I've already spoken with the sheriff. Thomas was here the night that poor girl was . . . hurt. Now please leave me be."

"Mrs. Garcia-Gonzales, we're not questioning your honesty, but you need to know another woman was murdered today, and we think another one has gone missing. If you can help us at all it may save a life."

There was no reply. Slowly the door opened three or four inches, a thick brass chain keeping it from opening wider. A woman probably in her early sixties peeked out. Her expression seemed resigned. "May I see some identification, please?"

"Of course." Cid and Tally handed her their ID cards through the small opening.

She inspected both carefully and then slipped the chain and fully opened the door, allowing the detectives to enter. Tally noted that besides the chain, the door had double locks.

The entry spilled into a large living room filled with windows and big oak ceiling beams. Walls were painted eggshell white, the carpet a light cream. French doors opened to the patio. Wall decorations were Asian, and rattan baskets with artificial water lilies lined the sandstone fireplace. Aromatic cooking fragrances from a late meal hung in the air, and Cid happily observed several ceramic ashtrays on various tables. There was a picture of George W. Bush on the entry wall. Tally couldn't figure that.

The woman who greeted them matched Tally's five-nine height. Braided flaxen hair held tightly in place by an expensive gold clip was pulled tightly back from her face and made her appear more youthful than she was.

Awkward and somewhat embarrassed, she shifted the front of her lavender silk robe as she ushered them into the step-down living room. "Whom do you represent?" she asked.

"Haskall's mother," Cid answered quietly.

She seated them in Chinese red low-back chairs.

Tally observed her closely. She was attractive, but not a regal beauty. Generous mouth, deep dimples, big hazel eyes with lids that drooped from age and creased, yet lovely porcelain complexion. Even in the tented robe, it was obvious she had retained her youthful figure. She was not, however, the woman pictured on Thomas's living room and basement walls.

An unspoken thought passed between Cid and Tally as the older woman seated herself on a lengthy beige couch.

"Your home is lovely," Tally said appreciatively, wondering how a phone company employee could afford such luxury. She took out her notebook and flipped several pages. "You are Mrs. Garcia-Gonzales?"

"Yes." She donned a pair of wire-rimmed glasses and seemed more at ease, wearing the expression of someone taught to speak only when spoken to. "Thomas's father and I are still married, although we have lived separately for a number of years. This is our home."

Her words were slightly slurred, giving both Tally and Cid the impression she suffered from a speech impediment or was a little drunk.

Retrieving a vintage fifties silver cigarette case from her pocket, she snapped it open and gracefully placed a Marlboro Light in her mouth, lighting it with a matching silver lighter. She scooted forward and blinked as she looked over the top of her glasses. "Would you care for a drink?" She gestured toward a glass-topped sideboard brimming with decanters.

"Of course," Cid said happily. She was on her feet before Mrs. Garcia-Gonzales could struggle off the couch. "Please relax. May I get you something?"

Drawing deeply on her cigarette, she looked at Cid brightly. "A small glass of Merlot. You'll find an open bottle on the counter along with glasses." She nodded at Tally.

"Nothing, thank you."

Studying a portrait of a fisherman in a skiff, Tally pointed. "Is that your work?"

"Oh my, no," she answered in a high-pitched voice. "Thomas's mother painted that."

Tally looked at her for a moment, then slowly shook her head. "But I thought . . ."

"I'm the second Mrs. Garcia-Gonzales. Mary. Francesca was the painter and divine musician."

Feeling an undertone to her words, Tally leaned forward waiting for more.

Cid set the Merlot on a wooden coaster and took a sip of the scotch she had poured herself. Mary Garcia-Gonzales smiled, lifted the wine to her lips, and drank half the glass.

"I'm not a talkative woman, especially to strangers." She looked at her watch. Annoyance crept into her eyes as she looked up. "As I said, I've told the sheriff everything I know." She paused, then added tersely, "I'm afraid you've made a trip out here for no reason."

The room was silent, as if someone had tossed the gauntlet.

"You said Francesca *was* the painter? She's dead?"

"Oh, my, yes. She died years ago. When Thomas was still a child."

Tally could not hide her surprise. "But he speaks of her as if she were here now."

"Jesus," Cid said, and took another sip of scotch.

Mary Garcia-Gonzales leaned forward toward Tally, wine-glass in one hand, cigarette in the other. She smiled without joy. "Thomas is an odd one. For as long as I've known him, he's been strange. I don't know if it was his mother's death or if he was simply born eccentric."

"Hah! Eccentric?" Cid sat down pulling her cigarettes from her pocket. "I assume that's your polite way of saying he's a nut-case. His cheese has not only slipped off the cracker, it fell on the floor. He probably was born deviant, and all these innocent women are suffering because of it."

The statement seemed to throw Mary Garcia-Gonzales off balance. She winced, then closed her eyes. For a time, Tally thought she was through talking, then Mary began to speak.

"I'm sorry."

"Sorry?" Tally asked.

She snuffed her cigarette in the ashtray. "Thomas's father, Felipe, and I tried so hard. We loved him. We took him to ball games and on family camping trips." She looked pale now. "After he hurt our neighbor's animals we all went for counseling, but it didn't help him."

She sipped her wine, set it on the coaster, and looked at Cid. "Maybe you're right. Maybe he was born evil."

The words stung Tally's heart. Silently she wondered, nurture or nature?

Mary propped her chin on one hand, glancing at Tally. "You said another poor woman was killed?"

Tally nodded.

"And you think Thomas is responsible?"

Again Tally nodded.

As if slapped, comprehension hit her. "Oh, God, what have we done?" She stared at the floor.

Aware Mary Garcia-Gonzales was not a woman to be pushed, Tally and Cid remained silent. It was as if in her loneliness Mary sought friendship, but was afraid to trust.

"Someone else is missing?"

"Evidence suggests it's a strong possibility," Tally answered in a flat voice.

"What do you expect from me?"

"Full disclosure. We need his history so we can understand what's motivating him. And more importantly we need to know where he is."

Mary picked up her glass of wine, took another sip. "I haven't seen him for weeks. Not since he came asking for an alibi." She spread her hands. "He can be very charming and persuasive and also terrifying. Like Felipe, I'm afraid of Thomas."

She finished her wine and set the glass down. Her eyes widened. "Maybe it's time," she said with painful honesty, "the family secrets were given a little air."

Tally's face hardened, her anger in check. "You said Thomas asked for an alibi? He wasn't with you the night Johanna Haskall's body was disposed?"

Mary seemed to flush and took a moment to compose her thoughts. "When will this information be made public?"

Cid lit her cigarette, let it dangle from her mouth. "If he's guilty of a crime, once he's been formally charged."

"When will that happen?"

Cid shrugged. "Ten minutes ago if I had my way. First, we

135

gotta catch him in the act or find some damn convincing hard evidence against him. The stuff we found so far is incriminating, pictures in his basement and hair on the wall, but it's not hard evidence. His attorney could say anyone plastered those to the wall. We need enough for the DA to file charges. Lady, he's not just good at what he does, he's extraordinary. He's going to be tough to nab. Unless, like I said, we catch him in the act. Or by some chance he's innocent."

"But you said there was another dead woman. Someone missing?" The conversation seemed to fluster Mary. She looked around the room as if answers were written on the wall. As if something was said that she could not accept.

Cid softened her voice. "It's one thing to know in your gut that someone has done something wrong, but it's an entirely different issue to be able to prove it in court." She shifted forward. Smiled a little. "I know this isn't easy for you. If we owe you an apology for being too blunt or cynical, then we're sorry. I'm afraid our past experiences create their own prejudices. Believe me, we are trying to be fair and give Thomas the benefit of doubt."

Folding her hands in front of her, Mary Garcia-Gonzales sat motionless. "I just want to be sure whatever I tell you tonight . . . that Thomas won't know it came from me." She opened her hands and wiped her palms on her robe.

Tally tilted her head. "Assuming Thomas is arrested, he will know nothing of the evidence until there's a hearing. Murder is a capital crime, so if bail was set I would imagine the sum would be out of Thomas's reach. Meaning he would be in jail until he's judged guilty or innocent. I also believe if your security was an issue, the police would provide you with some form of protection."

Shoulders relaxing some, Mary glanced at Tally. "Thomas came to me the morning of July sixth. Very early. I remember the date because it's Felipe's birthday and the time because I was just leaving for work. Ten past seven. He told me if the authorities questioned me I was to say he had been with me on the fifth from the time I got home from work until the next morning."

"And you agreed to this without question?" Tally asked.

Mary drew a silent breath. "Yes."

"Lip service," Cid said sarcastically, flicking a long ash into the ashtray. Her eyes lacked expression. What motivated people's actions had long ago ceased to surprise her.

"Good alibis are hard to come by. There's more than a few bank robbers serving hard time that wouldn't mind having their attorneys call you as a witness." Raw amusement now flashed in Cid's eyes. "You know, new evidence, new trial. I mean who the hell cares if what you say is fact or fiction and that a felon keeps roaming the streets. You just didn't have the balls to rat out the lousy bastard." She used the crude statement purposely to further unsettle Mary.

"You're nasty."

Cid gave her a cool look. "On my good days."

Mary threw up her hands, turned to Tally, her voice chilled. "Don't patronize me. How can you know anything of me? There are a thousand reasons why I respond in the way I do, and you'll never be privy to most of them," she shot back. Abruptly she stopped and looked into Cid's eyes, trying not to face the consequences her actions had caused. "Part of me hates Thomas for what he has done. The other part hates me for not being able to control or correct his actions.

"When Thomas was in high school I spent a week and a half in the hospital. My spleen was removed, the result of several well-placed punches from Thomas. I had told his principal he had cut classes and spent the day shooting rabbits with his twenty-two. He saw that as betrayal."

She sat back, took out another cigarette, and held it between her long tapered fingers. She gave a weary shrug. "A year and a half later, he beat his father to a bloody pulp when he refused to allow Thomas the use of the family car for a date with one of our farmhand's daughters. That decision was made only after his father had found blood in the car from a previous night out. We later learned he had raped his date."

She lit her cigarette, hands shaking. "There were other instances. Broken ribs. Smashed fingers. Accidents at the farm." She continued to look at Cid, voice bitter. "I'm afraid of Thomas. I did what I had to do. If he knew I was talking with you, I have no doubt he would hurt me seriously." She paused. "Or even worse, kill me."

"If Thomas wanted you dead"—Cid looked at her with a piercing stare—"we wouldn't be having this conversation now."

There was a note of confusion in Cid's voice. "Thomas clearly has issues. Probably pathological. Why didn't you have him arrested?"

"He was our son."

Mary removed her glasses and cleaned them using her robe. "Unfortunately we can't choose family. We accept both the good and the bad and do the best we can with it. We're all just trying to survive, aren't we?"

Bent forward, Tally watched Mary Garcia-Gonzales. She assessed her. A woman trapped by the past and afraid of the future. She was neither simple or stupid, but she was strong and determined. "Have you seen Thomas since the sixth of July?"

"No." She stopped herself and gazed across the room at a vase filled with fresh carnations. "He won't come back unless he needs another favor or learns I betrayed him."

"And his father," Tally asked, "will he bother Felipe?"

Mary got up, walked to the side table, and poured herself another glass of wine. She nodded at Cid.

Cid looked at her near empty glass and debated. "No thanks. I've had enough for now."

"Felipe," Mary began, "has lived out of the country for the

last four years. Costa Rica. Thomas thinks his father left me and just disappeared. That's not the case. We carefully planned everything. He comes home every couple of months to see me and take care of business here. He stays at a small apartment in Hollister. A place unknown to Thomas. Felipe is a good and loving man. He didn't deserve a son like . . ."

Mary did not have to finish. Cid could hear her helplessness. "I don't know who would," she offered with a mix of sympathy and distain. "It's a shame his father left you alone to deal with the consequences."

"Most people don't deserve what happens to them," Tally added. "Robbery, murder, auto accidents, adultery. Fortunately whatever wrongs we commit in our defense don't necessarily make us past hope. Maybe it's a hard-learned lesson, a warning of how to act or respond the next time someone betrays us."

A bleak understanding flashed in Mary's eyes. Then she drifted away, lost in memory. "Several years ago, when Thomas returned from traveling in South America, he demanded money from Felipe. My husband offered to give him a job but told him there was no freeloading. That night the main barn at the farm burned to the ground. Thousands and thousands of dollars were lost in product and productivity. A week later one of our managers was seriously injured by a piece of faulty equipment. An investigation determined bolts had been manually loosened, causing the accident. The following week a little girl disappeared. A migrant worker's daughter."

For a long time Mary was quiet, remembering. Then she turned her blue eyes to Cid and Tally. "Juanita Perez. Just five years old. She was never heard from again, and her body was never found."

She sat down; her voice had a strange edge. "Three days later I found our neighbor's little girl tied up in Thomas's closet. She had been beaten, sexually abused, and left to die." She sat back, bowed her head. "Felipe and I were devastated.

We paid the medical bills and arrived at a settlement with the family in exchange for their silence."

Tally considered her. She knew a sexual predator's behavior developed in their late teens or early twenties. "And Thomas?"

Shrugging, Mary shook her head. Then a concession. "We didn't always make good decisions. In retrospect he probably should have been sent away for treatment, or at least the authorities should have been notified."

Another of life's hard-learned lessons, Tally thought.

"The next day Felipe agreed to give Thomas a monthly stipend. Peace returned to the farm, and my husband decided to move his business to Costa Rica."

She took two sips of wine. "Neither Thomas nor the authorities are aware the farm in Gilroy was sold over a year ago. Nor that our house was sold confidentially the end of last month. I closed on the sale just yesterday. And my retirement becomes effective in two weeks. Felipe and I have so few years left, we want to live them peacefully and without fear. So you see I won't be here to give evidence against Thomas or"—she looked directly at Cid—patience strained, "any bank robbers."

Tally gave a wry smile and shook her head in silent understanding. Secrets piled on secrets until the weight was more than anyone could bear. A sad history of loss, guilt, regret. Rising, she crossed the room to the French doors and stared out at the wooden deck. A metal wind chime played a happy tune that did not fit the moment. "How did Francesca die?"

"She drowned."

"I thought she was a world-class swimmer. Olympic material," Tally said, watching Mary's reflection in the glass.

Inhaling deeply, Mary let the smoke slowly trickle from her nose. "She was. Felipe said she constantly tested herself. Confused challenge with likeability. Perfection with self-worth. That's why she was so superb with her music and art."

"Another neurotic Van Gogh?" Tally raised an eyebrow.

"She was sick. Had been her entire married life. And probably before. She saw a psychiatrist daily. Near the end she was only communicating with Thomas. Their relationship was so twisted. Her family was left out, as was Felipe. My husband said she only understood manipulation and dominance."

"And the day she died?"

"It was stormy and the Pacific surf was rugged. Not only were the waves large and hard to navigate, but the undertow was intense. She and her sister Gertrude had a bet that she couldn't swim out to the lighthouse and back within thirty minutes. A perfect challenge for Francesca's athletic ability. And perfect insanity." She drew her knees up and hugged them tightly with her arms, then let them fall back to the floor. Her movement had a certain grace.

"They found her body washed up against the rocks at dusk. Years later Thomas told me her skin was blue and icy cold. He said he touched her and lay beside her trying to warm her until the authorities made him move."

"Where did this happen?" Cid asked, dreading what she knew she was about to hear.

Crossing and re-crossing her legs, Mary Garcia-Gonzales gathered herself. There was a stillness in the room. "Goldenrod. Hughes Cove."

Tally staggered slightly as she turned to face Mary and examined her face. "What?"

"The Rogers family, Francesca's parents, owned a large vacation cottage just outside of town. She and Thomas spent most of the summer there. In the beginning, Felipe joined them on weekends when he wasn't harvesting, but the last few years of their marriage he stayed at the farm. Slept and ate his meals with the workers. He rarely saw Thomas or Francesca."

With barely suppressed anger Tally realized if Mary Garcia-

Gonzales had been forthright with the sheriff and shared this information sooner, Stella Fielding would probably still be alive.

"Where was Thomas when Francesca drowned? And how old was he?" Tally asked looking down at Mary.

Face impassive, Mary seemed to drift away. "Eleven, and he was standing on the bluffs with his aunt. He saw the whole thing." The vein in her temple seemed to throb; her voice filled with regret. "It was a sisterly bet. The sort of challenge Francesca was incapable of declining. If she won, Gertrude would go home for the summer and leave the vacation cottage to just Francesca and Thomas. If she lost, she would cut her hair short."

"Watching his mother die is probably what damaged him. Sent him over the edge." Cid pursed her lips and shook her head.

"I don't think so." Mary leaned forward and crushed her cigarette in the ashtray. She seemed a little puzzled, as if total understanding was out of her reach.

"From what Felipe said, they had a very strange relationship long before Francesca's death."

"Can you enlighten us?" Cid asked evenly.

Giving a reluctant nod, she picked up her wineglass and drained it. It was as if the alcohol created an emotional barrier.

"I knew Francesca long before I met Felipe. I volunteered for the San Jose Art Council. The board recognized Francesca's talent. They knew she had the potential to become an international star. But like Sylvia Plath, she had such a dark side, and they were afraid to promote her. With limited funds they couldn't afford to make a mistake." She waved her hand. "I don't believe she ever had a real showing of her work. Not with an art dealer of any reputation. I know she sold a painting now and then, but certainly she wasn't making a living.

"The first time I really spoke to her was at a luncheon given

142

by the chamber of commerce. There were several young women there with their children. Francesca spoke of how fond she was of little girls and how she hoped to have a dozen someday. She said girls were saintly. Perfect angels.

"I didn't see her again for a number of years. Then I bumped into her at a concert in the park. She introduced me to her four-year-old daughter, Tuscan. I never forgot the name because it was so beautiful. Our conversation was brief, and I didn't see her again."

Almost absently, Mary glanced at her empty glass. "It was years later that Felipe told me Tuscan was Thomas dressed as a girl."

"What?" For Tally the admission was as bizarre to hear as it must have been for Mary Garcia-Gonzales to speak.

Mary's recounting was now calm and introspective, and there was a deep sadness to her voice as she continued.

"Thomas attended Saint Patrick's Elementary school. Fortunately Francesca took him to a different parish for Mass. When it was time for his First Communion, she forbid the family to attend. Felipe learned later that Thomas had worn a dress and little Mary Jane shoes as he apparently did whenever he attended service."

She hunched over, fighting the need to cry. Her body trembled, her voice laced with contempt. "He was only seven. Francesca had instructed him never to use the restrooms, but with the excitement of the day he found he couldn't wait. He became confused as to which toilet to use, men's or women's. He went to the priest and asked for help. The good father was of the old school and flew into a rage. In front of all the children waiting to parade into the church, he walked Thomas to the door and told him to go home and never return. Christian idealism at work," she added dryly.

Flushed with anger, Mary continued. "Francesca was beside herself. She made Thomas recite one hundred Hail Marys kneeling on the cement patio, and then she took him to the ballpark where his friends were playing and marched him up and down the baseline in his dress. She made him promise never to disobey her again." Tears rippled down her full, ashen cheeks. "He never did."

The room was silent with sadness. Cid bent her head. Tally stared blankly at Mary Garcia-Gonzales. The deeper she dug into this case, the more complicated it became. Her voice was firm now. "Where was Felipe when all of this was going on?"

"He had a business to run."

"The hell," Cid said, something heartbreaking in her tone. "He had a son to raise."

Mary Garcia-Gonzales seemed troubled now, though whether by recognition of her husband's neglect or Francesca's cruelty, Tally could not tell.

"Why is it," Mary began slowly, "the chaste always end up judged? The marriage was a house of cards. Francesca controlled Thomas and allowed Felipe only limited contact. She made all the calls. Try as Felipe may, she wanted Thomas for herself. He even shared her bed. She would play an old Gershwin tune on the piano, *Somebody loves you, I wonder who,* and then sing it to Thomas. It was her signal, and they would go off to the bedroom alone."

Tally gave a grimace, sat back, edgy now. She could no longer fight off the terrible visualization, the repugnance of Thomas's childhood. "They were having sex? He was just a little boy."

"I'm not sure, no one was. But it's a pretty good guess something seamy was going on." The statement seemed inadequate for the probable consequences.

Mary drew a breath. "Felipe wanted to be a good father, only his influence came too late to repair the damage Francesca had already inflicted.

"And as for Thomas, you seem quite closed." Her patience seemed to be fraying. There was almost a fury behind her words as if she had flip-flopped on her opinion of who Thomas really was. "You are assuming too much. It's as if you have singled him out. You don't seem to have any other suspects. Thomas may not be the ideal son, but surely there's a possibility of his innocence regarding these dreadful crimes."

The statement did not call for an immediate answer, so Tally gave none. Her mind had already moved forward.

"Who identified Francesca's body?"

"Thomas."

Tally's gaze was without understanding. "The authorities took the word of an eleven-year-old mentally wounded boy?"

In the brightly lit room, Mary studied her. Her face held contempt. "Detective, I wasn't there, and I'm not responsible for what happened at that time. Goldenrod is a small village. Perhaps the police weren't or aren't as vigilant as you are accustomed to. For all I know, several people could have identified her body."

"You're right. I'm sorry," Tally said, her sympathy real. The defensiveness she saw in Mary not only ran deep but had become survivor behavior. She shook her head and slapped herself mentally. "It's been hard on you, hasn't it?"

Looking at her out of the corner of her eye, Mary nodded, her voice tightening. "In many, many ways. Rumors. Frightened friends and colleagues. Disgruntled family."

Tally waited, then cautiously asked, "Did Felipe eventually see Francesca's body?"

"No." Mary got up and poured herself yet another glass of wine. Her shoulders sagged as her white feathered slippers slid silently across the rug. This time she did not offer Cid or Tally a drink. "Francesca was cremated immediately after the autopsy. There wasn't a service. No eulogies."

A ripple of concern hit Tally. "So, other than Thomas's word, it may or may not have been Francesca Garcia-Gonzales who died in the surf that day?"

Mary's face turned to chalk. "I suppose that's a possibility. Although I can't begin to imagine why Francesca would fabricate her own death. And Gertrude, Francesca's older sister, was there."

"Is she still alive?"

Mary waited for a moment. Took her seat. "As far as I know." She pushed her wire-rimmed glasses up the bridge of her nose.

"Does Thomas still see her?"

She shrugged and seemed hesitant to answer. "The more we talk the less comfortable I am knowing that I may be responsible for Thomas's incarceration." She jabbed her finger into her palm. "Felipe is my husband, and Thomas is his son. We've protected him all his life. Right or wrong, I can't abide with changing that now. I can't go against what I know to be my husband's wishes. Besides, who are you that I owe any explanation?" She fought for dignity.

Tally squinted in suspicion. To think of a predator like Thomas running loose one more day, one more hour, made her blood run cold. "Would it help you, Mrs. Garcia-Gonzales, if I told you we found chains and shackles in Thomas's basement tonight? That there was blood and hair imbedded in the brick and pictures of victims plastered on the wall. Photos of little girls and innocent women? We don't want to burn Thomas at the stake, but surely you see where this is going? We've got a body count."

Shuddering, Mary nearly spilled her wine. She opened her mouth to speak and then could not, as if her thoughts were too grim to face.

Cid set her glass down, stood, and walked past Tally to the French doors, opening one. She let the breeze blow across her warm face for a few seconds and then quietly shut the door. "Whether you know it or not, Mary, we're the best friends you've got right now. The sooner we catch Thomas, the easier and safer your life is gonna be."

Tally could almost see the silent battle of conscience.

"I hope to God I never regret this, my loyalty should be to family," Mary Garcia-Gonzales said at last, sullen and a little confused.

"Gertrude Rogers lives about ten miles from here. An area still considered country. And although she was intimately involved in Francesca's death, she blamed Felipe. Said if he had loved Francesca more, her sister never would have taken such grave risks. Still Gertrude's guilt was deep, and she felt it was her obligation to keep the memory of Thomas's mother alive for him."

She gave a chuckle. "Before high school, he used to run away to her house when he got mad at Felipe and me. He spent hours in Gertrude's old wine room. It was his sanctuary, and only he had the keys to the door. He used to tell me about his clever inventions that he constructed there, but I knew there were other things that went on, too. For certain he had Francesca's old gun. A ghastly thing, black with a long barrel. I used to wonder what or who he had there in that cold dark room, but finally I figured if it didn't bother Gertrude, it shouldn't eat at me."

Tally caught a hint of dislike.

"About six years ago, Gertrude came to me." Mary pulled her legs up again, seemed to hug her knees tighter. "The side of her face was black and blue, nearly purple. And the fingers on one hand were splinted. It was so obvious she needed to talk, but it was equally apparent that Thomas owned her. She commented on my garden and our home and then left, her needs not voiced. I've haven't seen her since. Out of kindness and I suppose some denial, I never called her. But I do know Thomas spends a great deal of time at her house. Her neighbor is a former colleague and friend of mine. He called just yesterday, after he'd gotten back from Goldenrod. He said Thomas had asked him to pick him up there twice in the last several months. If Thomas is in trouble or trying to hide, you'll find him at Gertrude's."

She made a steeple of her fingers and stared vacantly across the room. "Francesca wanted a saint, an angel," she said absently.

"Well, she raised a sinner," Tally quietly replied, her smile cold.

Chapter Fifteen
Thursday, September 17
12:45 a.m.

Nestled in thick trees, a mix of redwood, pine, and fir, Gertrude Rogers's street lay just west of the Monte Bello Mountain Ridge and ran parallel with Skyline Boulevard.

The sky remained clear. The stars seemed close enough to pluck, the moon a white Frisbee gliding slowly along its charcoal path. The air had the clean, fresh scent of storm afterglow.

Her modest gray wooden house, built in the 1920s, had a small porch surrounded by flower beds that had fallen into ne glect. Large flower pots had been moved, leaving weeds to sprout where they once had been. The lawn was unmowed and heavily invaded with crabgrass. Like Gertrude, the house had survived numerous earthquakes, drought, deluge, and even an occasional freak snowstorm. Tally realized the area was isolated just enough to make murder invisible.

A white Toyota Camry sat in the driveway. Thomas's car.

Tally wondered if Thomas was watching. Dousing her headlights, she pulled forward off the road, a gravelly spot hidden by trees about a hundred yards from Gertrude Rogers's front door. The car dropped forward as both front tires sank into a deep rut and then bounced back, the crunching sound of tires over stones echoing down the dank, empty road.

"Now what?" Cid asked. She could almost feel Thomas's presence—ominous, sinister, and menacing. "You know we're executing a search without a warrant?"

Studying Cid's face, Tally shrugged and crossed her arms. "We're private, we don't need a warrant or even probable cause."

Cid smiled a little. "That's twice in one night we're breaking and entering. That bother you?"

On the surface Tally knew they were partners exchanging thoughts. But it also felt to Tally like Cid was giving a warning that they were dangerously close to crossing the line of criminal activity. She chose to ignore the question.

Playing it all through in her mind, she hadn't imagined things going down this way. She thought it would be days or weeks before they uncovered Johanna Haskall's killer. She debated calling the sheriff or Chief Peterson, but what could she say? *We think Thomas Garcia-Gonzales is a serial killer? He might have had a woman shackled in his basement? We're guessing he has a victim at Gertrude Rogers's house?* Those kinds of unfounded accusations would make both her and Cid as popular as a skunk at a family barbecue, to say nothing of what it would do to their future credibility. But what concerned her most was that they were simply running out of time as his killing timetable grew shorter. And then there was the gnawing possibility that Francesca Garcia-Gonzales was still alive and masterminding Thomas's every move. He had to obey.

She slid forward in the car seat, her hand moving to the butt of her Glock. She unsnapped the lock strap and scanned the shadowed forest and dark road. There was no sign of movement, but then Thomas was very good at hiding.

"Did you notice any lights on?" she finally asked Cid.

"No, but if he's in the wine room, his sanctuary, as Mary Garcia-Gonzales called it, there probably wouldn't be any visible light from the street. And at this hour I would guess Gertrude Rogers would be sleeping."

"Do you think he's got someone in there with him?" Tally asked, her adrenaline pumping.

Cid was quiet for the moment. "I'd hafta guess he ain't playing solitaire."

Tally's eyes shut. "Taking another woman, moving so quickly, what do you think his motive is?"

"Hell, take your pick." Cid's voice was hollow. "He's emotionally disturbed. Damaged. Probably sexually abused. Ordinary motives don't necessarily hold with that kind of background. We've flushed him out so he's a loose cannon at this point."

Pushing her hands back over her hair, Tally felt the strangeness of life. The story of Thomas Garcia-Gonzales was a true tragedy. Whether he was born with lousy genes or his twisted mother molded him into a monster, she didn't know. Perhaps she hoped for too much and saw the better side of people most of the time. But she was sure that she didn't want Katie involved in this mess, and she didn't want Francesca Garcia-Gonzales still among the living.

In the darkness, Tally's profile was still. "I'm concerned for Katie." The guilt was clearly written across her face. "I should have gone home as soon as she told me Thomas had called the hospital."

Glancing at her watch, Cid seemed surprised by the admission. Impulsively she rested her hand on Tally's shoulder. "You can't cover all your bases at once. If you try, it'll eat you up inside. Katie's no dummy, Tal. You warned her. She understands. And can keep herself safe."

She pulled her arm back and looked at her watch again. "It's a quarter to one. You spoke to Katie sometime around eleven-thirty. Thomas would have had to bust his balls to get to San Francisco and back here in such a short time frame. Hell, he'd a had to fly. Drive time alone makes it a near impossibility. It's close to an hour's trip one way. Besides, it takes time, Tal, to abduct someone. I mean, Katie wouldn't just give up without a fight."

With dim moonlight sifting through the windshield, Tally's eyes watched her. "Naw." Cid shook her head. "If there's someone with him, it ain't Katie."

Her fingertips clasped to the edge of the steering wheel, Tally heard the crickets and saw the tree shadows fall across the hood of the car. She didn't want to let her emotions get in the way of the investigation, but her gut was screaming at her, and she needed to listen. She picked up her cell. After five rings the voice mail clicked on. Suddenly Tally felt cold.

Skin tingling, Cid gazed at Tally, the whites of her eyes red with fatigue. "She's probably in the shower."

There was a part of Tally's brain that knew she was being irrational, but there also was the suppressed guilt. "I couldn't live with myself if anything ever happened to Katie because of my neglect. Maybe worry is my penance for being a workaholic."

Tally looked out the window at nothing. Her voice tensed. "Francesca would have had plenty of time to make the trip to San Francisco and back here." She gazed sharply at Cid before opening the door. "Let's move."

"You know," Tally whispered, looking across the roof of the BMW, "I almost feel sorry for Thomas."

Cid shut the car door, the click barely audible. "Well don't." She was a cop, with a cop's candid way of thinking, and the truth was that Thomas had probably killed, and he had to pay the price for his actions. Her voice was rough with quiet anger. "It's an imperfect world. There's a million poor souls out there who had rotten childhoods, and none of them turned into serial killers."

Tally felt the hollow cynicism, the residue of a retired cop. She looked into Cid's tired, hard face and slowly nodded. Softly she said, "I'm glad Mimi will be here soon." She pulled her flashlight from the backseat floor and slid it in her pocket and closed her door.

Slowly, cautiously, they walked to the back of the car. The eerie quiet seemed to push Tally's thoughts back to the case, away from her concern for Katie.

"And by the way, the positions the bodies were left in at Hughes Cove?" She paused, waiting for Cid to look up. "I put it together while Mary Garcia-Gonzales was talking. They're all swimming. Stroke for stroke. One arm up. One arm down."

For a second Cid's eyes widened. She swatted at a mosquito. "Crazy world."

The ground was uneven, filled with blistered and scarred tree roots that had been exposed by erosion. Twigs slapped at their faces and tiny branches snapped under their weight, sending an imagined booming resonance across the property. The air was still.

Their shoes collected mud and muck and were squishy with rainwater from the grass and tall weeds.

Both Tally and Cid stumbled several times before reaching the outer perimeter of the house. Silently and carefully they made their way to the back. Tally's heart pounded too fast and too hard in her ears, and Cid's legs quivered from exhaustion.

A dim glow of light from a solitary window filtered through a stalk of fern and came to rest on the grass. The remainder of the house was dark. They stopped, crouched. The smell of mold and dampness surrounded them. Senses sharp, Tally positioned herself so she could see the corner of the house and the wine room window.

They heard conversation, the volume rising and falling, but could not see through the dirty, mud-splattered window. Then a scream. Muffled, not filled with terror, but a scream.

Tally dropped to her knees, her head at window level.

"Thomas, darling, put the knife down and finish your sewing."

"Yes, Mother."

Tally leaned closer to the window, rubbed a small amount of dirt from the corner, and peered inside. Thomas was standing there, staring steadily down at his captive. Her arms limply cuffed and hanging above her head, her face already a maze of broken blood vessels and discolored skin. A pile of chopped hair surrounded her naked torso.

It was not Katie, but whoever it was, she was obviously in deep distress. Tally felt a new horror.

Somehow Thomas seemed bigger. Thicker across the shoulders. Maybe it was because his latest victim sat helpless and small beside him. He was wearing a black silk shirt with white tie. *Dressed for murder*, she thought.

He raised a gun, waved it in front of the young woman. From the description Mary Garcia-Gonzales had given, Tally guessed it probably was Francesca's old gun. A 360 Magnum.

"You must obey," a woman said with a mixture of impatience and concern attached to her voice.

Tally scanned as much of the cement room as she could see, but could not tell where the sound had come from.

Meekly, Thomas laid the gun on a table next to a sewing machine.

Pushing to her feet, Tally ducked to the right, silently signaling Cid to follow. She found a side door and crouched, checking for inside movement, straining to hear over the crickets' musical violin. There was no sound from inside the house.

"Try the door," Cid instructed, dropping down behind Tally, her breathing coming in gasps.

Her fingers touched the knob, then turned. "Locked." She pulled her wallet from her khakis, removed a credit card, and slipped it at an angle just above the latch to catch the edge of the lock. Softly she pushed. The door did not budge. She repositioned the credit card. Shut her eyes and concentrated. Fingers straining, she jiggled it and then allowed the card to slide slowly. She felt a catch. There was a click, and the half-rotted door opened. One thing good about being an ex-cop, she had learned the tricks of the criminal trade.

The room was pitch-black, and she wasn't sure where they were. She reached for her flashlight and realized she must have dropped it somewhere outside. It was cold and still, the air stale. She waited, listened, tried to hear past the sound of her own breathing. Something rubbed against her leg. Tally swallowed. Sweat beaded on her forehead. She knelt, reached out, felt the soft fur of a cat. She ran her hand down its back, listened to the purring. The cat whipped its head from side to side and began pacing.

Eyes now adjusted to the dark, in the distance, Tally could barely make out an outline of light seeping from the cracks around an old and poorly hung door.

She signaled for Cid to stay put and then slowly and stealthily crawled across the floor, spreading her weight, fully aware that any heavy or loud movement could be easily heard by anyone down the hall.

When she got to the door, the low hum of a sewing machine crawled up the corridor.

Suddenly Thomas shouted, "I've finished, Mother, isn't it beautiful?"

Behind Tally, Cid moved in slowly, her hands out front,

blindly feeling her way. She tiptoed, waiting between steps, then felt a soft lump under the sole of her shoe an instant before the cat let out a scathing howl.

The corridor went silent.

Tally put her hand on the doorknob. She knew they had to move fast, before Thomas had more time to think. She flung open the door, snatched and cocked her Glock in one motion. Cid was right behind, her Smith and Wesson at her side.

The noxious smell nearly knocked both of them to their knees as they began their rapid descent down the long dark hall. Cid gagged, but kept her gun level and ready.

The foundation for the old house had been built with fairly large rocks and a series of flat stones. Mold and even a little moss grew up the walls. Five bare lightbulbs illuminated the damp and gloomy space. For the moment, the only sound was Cid's labored breathing.

The first thing Tally saw was the dark form of a body hanging in the corner. It looked like a side of beef in a meat locker, only this butcher's specialty was human.

Thomas sat next to his sewing machine, staring at them, staring at their guns. He was casual, unconcerned as if he had been expecting them. He spread his hands almost surrendering, the scrapes on his face from earlier in the evening still angry and red.

"Well surprise, surprise. Look who's here and at such a late hour." Water dripped in some far-off corner. "Meet my guest, Gloria Tynes."

Tally glanced at his captive. Suddenly high-pitched squeals escaped from the corners of her taped mouth. Her brown hair was crudely cut and her small, firm breasts encrusted with dried blood. And for the first time in hours, her exotic hazel eyes held hope.

"Put down the guns," he said in a tone that suggested this was a game of checkers, and it was his move.

Eyes not wavering, Tally kept her gun sighted on Thomas's head but said nothing. She wanted to shoot.

"Mother, we have guests. Rude guests. They don't obey."

Tally flinched and backed up beside Cid. She looked to the right then the left, listening for someone else. She heard nothing.

Thomas seemed to grow in confidence as he shifted his weight in his chair. "I said, put down the guns."

He raised his foot, rested it on the table next to his 360 Magnum. A strap was tethered to his ankle and then to a soft rope. Tally's eyes followed the cord to the ceiling just in front of Gloria. A long, heavily weighted sword-like blade resembling a trapeze was balanced on two pieces of metal. A lever to the side was attached to the rope. Tally's whole body trembled, the gun in her hand now visibly shaking.

Thomas smiled. Chuckled. "Ingenious, isn't it?"

Cid looked up, but her view was blocked by a post.

"It's a swinging guillotine. I built it when I was sixteen. Killing is such fun." He reached down and touched the strap on his ankle. "One yank and Gloria becomes a distant memory. I don't think you want that on your conscience."

He leaned forward and picked up the Magnum. "Put down your guns. You move or shoot, she's dead." He jerked a thumb in Gloria's direction and pulled the hammer.

Cid moved toward him, her gun trained on the narrow spot between his bushy eyebrows.

He raised his arm. His look over the gun sight was filled with loathing. There was no hesitation.

The Magnum went off with a booming bang.

In the same instant Tally heard the report, Cid emitted a loud groan.

Gloria screeched, her body bucking on the table.

Cid's arm jerked up; her gun dropped to the cobbled floor and skipped end over end under the table. She staggered, eyes widening with astonishment.

By reflex Tally's eyes shut. A fine spew of blood dotted her gold sweatshirt and a faint mist, like spray paint, spread across her left cheek.

Bent over with pain, Cid grabbed her right wrist, trying to curb the discomfort. A thick stream of blood ran down her arm and soaked into her navy Dockers. "You're a piece of shit, Thomas."

"Did I forget to mention earlier this evening," Thomas said with visible rage, "that I was a crack shot. Another attribute I thought I would bring to police work. That is, until you, Cidney, blew my career, took away my chosen profession."

Tally took a step toward Cid, her anger shifting to fear as she looked at the bloody arm. She reached out.

"Put the gun down or your partner dies fast."

"I'm okay," Cid said, shaken, "it's just a flesh wound. Missed the bone."

The whole night was beginning to feel like Tally was in the presence of insanity. She didn't know whether to shoot or dive for cover. She looked at the guillotine, then Gloria and Cid. Involuntarily they all had become Thomas's prey. She forced herself not to turn on him and laid her Glock on the floor.

"Now kick it over here."

She did as she was told. She turned and walked back to Cid, pulling a handkerchief from her pocket and wrapping it around the wound, trying to stem the flow of blood.

Cid's face was white and unforgiving. Tally grabbed a rusted lawn chair from against the wall and helped her into the seat.

"Good." Thomas stood, picked up Tally's nine-millimeter and slid it into a drawer. He walked to Gloria, Magnum waving in one hand, brushing cut hair to the floor with the other.

Tally took an aggressive step forward, calculating the distance between her and Thomas. Everything was on fast forward and happening too fast. Déjà vu.

Smiling, Thomas pointed to the ceiling, gave his leg a little jerk. "Guillotine."

Tally stopped.

"Her hair was so lovely. I had to cut it," he said with an officious air, "otherwise she would have drowned, and then none of us would have had any fun."

"Thomas, I've told you a dozen times not to trust these detectives. Now you've given them one of our secrets." The voice was formal, yet alluring and seductive and seemed to be coming from the area where Thomas stood.

Tally felt like she had been touched by velvet as she again scanned the cellar, looking for the source of the voice. She looked closely at Thomas.

"I told you, Mother, I have it under control."

Withered in pain, Cid stared at Thomas then Tally, her chest heaving. "What the fuck?"

Tally shook her head as if to clear it. "Where's Gertrude?"

Assuming a certain calm, Thomas smiled, pointing to the corner. "In the fridge."

"Jesus Christ. Jesus H. Christ." Cid's voice drifted off.

"She's going to the crabs tomorrow. I have no use for her here. Dent provided me with everything I needed to finish my project."

He whirled and tripped over his feet.

Tally winced, looking at the guillotine rope as it first swayed, then grew taut.

"Be a damn shame if I fell." He smiled again, reached for a quilt on the sewing machine. He signaled for Tally to move closer. "Beautiful, isn't it."

Tally looked, then staggered. She saw the bonbons immediately. Bile rose in her throat as she struggled to retrieve some form of sensibility or understanding as suspicion moved to fact.

Tattoos cut from the bodies of human victims. Each square neatly trimmed, machine and hand stitched into Thomas's idea of an heirloom quilt.

Tally had no immediate response. Her mind felt heavy. The sight of a dead body, a captive, the stench, Cid's wound, made everything seem surreal. A corpse in a refrigerator. It was madness.

She began moving in on Thomas. Small steps. She tried to keep her mind clear, as if her life depended on it, and it did.

Feeling a revulsion she tried to hide, she made her voice light. Tried to think like Thomas. "It's beautiful." She pointed at the quilt. "Are you going to use it for decoration?"

Turning, he resumed viewing the quilt. His voice held impatience, as if he wanted Tally to understand. "No. It's to keep Mother warm." He glanced up, eyes watery. "She's blue with cold."

Thomas's face twisted. He looked at her as if trying to face something that was lost long ago. "If she had cut her hair she wouldn't have had to go swimming."

In a very soft baritone he began to sing. *Somebody loves me, I wonder who, I wonder who.*

"Thomas, that's enough." The voice was severe. "You must obey."

From deep in her throat, another alarmed squeal escaped Gloria Tynes.

Silent, Tally felt a chill on her skin. She turned to Cid. She could hardly breathe. The damage Francesca had done to Thomas involved far more than murder.

Thomas lowered his eyelids. When he looked up his face was soft. The look of shy embarrassment. The lines around his mouth curled into a gentle smile. He held out his hand. "I'm Francesca. Francesca Garcia-Gonzales. I'm sorry I have no makeup on. Usually when I'm with the girls, Thomas's captives, I wear makeup. And my hair"—he touched the top of his head—"I just haven't had time to brush it. Normally it's long and lovely and soft to the touch."

Hunched over in her chair, clutching her arm, Cid recoiled, then whispered, "Split personality." She chose her next words very carefully. "Your mother did you wrong, Thomas."

He raised his gun, bracing his wrist with his left hand. "Don't you say a word about my mother." His finger tightened on the trigger.

Tally lunged.

He fired. The gun jerked upward.

Falling forward, Cid slipped from the chair, her injured arm flopping on the floor.

With her full weight, Tally slammed her arm down across Thomas's hand, knocking the gun to the floor, her momentum pushing him backward onto the table, sprawling across Gloria's bare legs. Just as he rose, Tally's knees collapsed. She fell to the floor landing on the tethered rope.

There was a sickening lopping sound and then a chilling scream from Gloria as Thomas slid off the table and landed on the floor, beside Tally, his neck a gaping wound. His breathing gurgled and whistled as air escaped from the gash in his windpipe and spurts of blood colored his white tie crimson. He tried to raise his arm, but he had lost all strength. His lifeblood pooled at his shoulders, mixing with Gloria Tynes's discarded hair. His eyes twitched with confusion and surprise. Soon the shallow whistle gave way to silence.

Grabbing the Magnum, Tally half crawled, half swam across the room.

Like Thomas's tie, Cid's white shirt was slowly turning scarlet. Her eyes were open. In an odd moment of clarity, they seemed more blue and more peaceful than usual to Tally. Cid's smile was filled with warmth when she looked at her. Then slowly her lids shut as she said, "Mimi."

To be continued . . .

161

Publications from
BELLA BOOKS, INC.
The best in contemporary lesbian fiction

P.O. Box 10543, Tallahassee, FL 32302
Phone: 800-729-4992
www.bellabooks.com

WHEN LOVE FINDS A HOME by Megan Carter. 280 pp. What will it take for Anna and Rona to find their way back to each other again?   1-59493-041-4 $12.95

MEMORIES TO DIE FOR by Adrian Gold. 240pp. Rachel Katz, a forensic psychologist, attempts to avoid her attraction to the charms of Anna Sigurdson. Will Anna's persistence and patience get her past Rachel's fears of a broken heart?   1-59493-038-4 $12.95

SILENT HEART by Claire McNab. 280 pp. Exotic lesbian romance.
                                                        1-59493-044-9 $12.95

MIDNIGHT RAIN by Peggy J. Herring. 240 pp. Bridget McBee is determined to find the woman who saved her life.   1-59493-021-X $12.95

THE MISSING PAGE A Brenda Strange Mystery by Patty G. Henderson. 240 pp. Brenda investigates her client's murder . . .   1-59493-004-X $12.95

WHISPERS ON THE WIND by Frankie J. Jones. 240 pp. Dixon thinks she and her best friend, Elizabeth Colter, would make the perfect couple . . .   1-59493-037-6 $12.95

CALL OF THE DARK: EROTIC LESBIAN TALES OF THE SUPERNATURAL edited by Therese Szymanski—from Bella After Dark. 320 pp.   1-59493-040-6 $14.95

A TIME TO CAST AWAY A Helen Black Mystery by Pat Welch. 240 pp. Helen stops by Alice's apartment—only to find the woman dead . . .   1-59493-036-8 $12.95

DESERT OF THE HEART by Jane Rule. 224 pp. The book that launched the most popular lesbian movie of all time is back.   1-1-59493-035-X $12.95

THE NEXT WORLD by Ursula Steck. 240 pp. Anna's friend Mido is threatened and eventually disappears . . .   1-59493-024-4 $12.95

CALL SHOTGUN by Jaime Clevenger. 240 pp. Kelly gets pulled back into the world of private investigation . . .   1-59493-016-3 $12.95

52 PICKUP by Bonnie J. Morris and E.B. Casey. 240 pp. 52 hot, romantic tales—one for every Saturday night of the year.   1-59493-026-0 $12.95

GOLD FEVER by Lyn Denison. 240 pp. Kate's first love, Ashley, returns to their home town, where Kate now lives . . .   1-1-59493-039-2 $12.95

RISKY INVESTMENT by Beth Moore. 240 pp. Lynn's best friend and roommate needs her to pretend Chris is his fiancé. But nothing is ever easy.   1-59493-019-8 $12.95

HUNTER'S WAY by Gerri Hill. 240 pp. Homicide detective Tori Hunter is forced to team up with the hot-tempered Samantha Kennedy.   1-59493-018-X $12.95